DATE DUE

NOV 1 9 2014

APP

AN ENEMY WITHIN:

Overcoming
Cancer and Other
Life-Threatening
Diseases

AN ENEMY WITHIN:

Overcoming Cancer and Other Life-Threatening Diseases

Patricia Therrien

 Mason Crest Publishers

AN ENEMY WITHIN: Overcoming Cancer and Other
Life-Threatening Diseases

MASON CREST PUBLISHERS INC.
370 Reed Road
Broomall, Pennsylvania 19008
(866)MCP-BOOK (toll free)
www.masoncrest.com

Because the stories in this series are told by real people, in
some cases names have been changed to protect the privacy
of the individuals.

9 8 7 6 5 4 3 2
 ISBN 978-1-4222-0449-8 (series)
 ISBN 978-1-4222-1462-6 (series) (pbk.)

Library of Congress Cataloging-in-Publication Data

Therrien, Patricia.
  An enemy within : overcoming cancer and other life-
threatening diseases / by Patty Therrien.
      p. cm. — (Survivors: ordinary people, extraordinary
circumstances)
  Includes bibliographical references and index.
  ISBN 978-1-4222-0450-4   ISBN 978-1-4222-1463-3 (pbk.)
 1. Cancer in children—Patients—Biography—Juvenile
literature. 2. Catastrophic illness—Patients—Biography—
Juvenile literature. I. Title.
  RC281.C4.T465 2009
  362.196'99400922—dc22
                                              2008033776

Design by MK Bassett-Harvey.
Produced by Harding House Publishing Service, Inc.
www.hardinghousepages.com
Cover design by Wendy Arakawa.
Printed in The Hashimite Kingdom of Jordan.

CONTENTS

Introduction

Each of us is confronted with challenges and hardships in our daily lives. Some of us, however, have faced extraordinary challenges and severe adversity. Those who have lived—and often thrived—through affliction, illness, pain, tragedy, cruelty, fear, and even near-death experiences are known as survivors. We have much to learn from survivors and much to admire.

Survivors fascinate us. Notice how many books, movies, and television shows focus on individuals facing—and overcoming—extreme situations. *Robinson Crusoe* is probably the earliest example of this, followed by books like the *Swiss Family Robinson*. Even the old comedy *Gilligan's Island* appealed to this fascination, and today we have everything from the Tom Hanks' movie *Castaway* to the hit reality show *Survivor* and the popular TV show *Lost*.

What is it about survivors that appeals so much to us? Perhaps it's the message of hope they give us. These people have endured extreme challenges—and they've overcome them. They're ordinary people who faced extraordinary situations. And if they can do it, just maybe we can too.

This message is an appropriate one for young adults. After all, adolescence is a time of daily challenges. Change is everywhere in their lives, demanding that they adapt and cope with a constantly shifting reality. Their bodies change in response to increasing levels of sex hormones; their thinking processes change as their brains develop, allowing them to think in more abstract ways; their social lives change as new people and peers become more important. Suddenly, they experience the burning need to form their own identities. At the same time, their emotions are labile and unpredictable. The people they were as children may seem to have disappeared beneath the onslaught of new emotions, thoughts, and sensations. Young adults have to deal with every single one of these changes, all at the same time. Like many of the survivors whose stories are told in this series, adolescents' reality is often a frightening, confusing, and unfamiliar place.

Young adults are in crises that are no less real simply because these are crises we all live through (and most of us survive!) Like all survivors, young adults emerge from their crises transformed; they are not the people they were before. Many of them bear scars they will carry with them for life—and yet these scars can be integrated into their new identities. Scars may even become sources of strength.

In this book series, young adults will have opportunities to learn from individuals faced with tremendous struggles. Each individual has her own story, her own set of circumstances and challenges, and her own way of coping and surviving. Whether facing cancer or abuse, terrorism or natural disaster, genocide or school violence, all the survivors who tell their stories in this series have found the ability and will to carry on despite the trauma. They cope, persevere, persist, and live on as a person changed forever by the ordeal and suffering they endured. They offer hope and wisdom to young adults: if these people can do it, so can they!

These books offer a broad perspective on life and its challenges. They will allow young readers to become more self-aware of the demanding and difficult situations in their own lives—while at the same time becoming more compassionate toward those who have gone through the unthinkable traumas that occur in our world.

— Andrew M. Kleiman, M.D.

Chapter One

IMAGINE . . .

Imagine you have been told you won't be able to graduate at the end of the year with your class, or that after playing an entire season of basketball with your teammates you won't be in the playoffs. How would you feel if you were told you could attend the high school prom, but you couldn't dance? Or, that not only would you never be able to play soccer again or participate in a track meet, you would never, ever be able to run again? That while everybody else has aced their driver's test and been given occasional custody of the keys to the family car, you will continue to be chauffeured by your parents? Sounds like a pretty raw deal, doesn't it? Maybe even cruel and unusual punishment!

Now imagine that you've been diagnosed with a serious disease such as cancer, and the

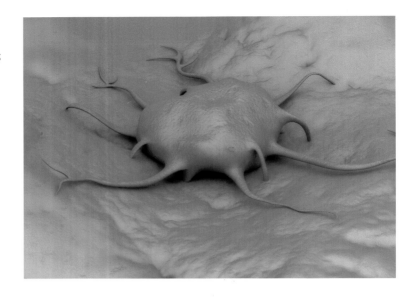

Cancer is caused by abnormal cells (like the one shown here) multiplying within the body.

reason you can't compete in that playoff game is that you are in a treatment room getting your weekly treatment instead. You can't run in the track meet, or in fact any track meet again, because part of the bone in your leg has been replaced with a metal rod. While your classmates are marching to "Pomp and Circumstance" at graduation, you are kept at a safe distance from the public at large because your blood counts—and therefore your immune system—are so suppressed you would be unable to fight off infections which could cause you to run dangerously high fevers and become seriously ill. You can't even consider learning to drive yet because one of the drugs you take causes your eyes to blur, making it very hard to focus and read the road signs. You sit out the prom, not because you are the classic version of a wallflower, but because the high-dose steroids you take have given you a case of osteoporosis that is worse than anything your grandmother could imagine. You have lost two inches of height because your vertebrae are so thin they have begun to compress. The bone in your hip has begun to die, making walking across a room excruciatingly painful, not to mention dancing!

Most of us like to think that it's only adults—and usually older adults—who get serious diseases like cancer. But the fact is, every year, 14 in every 100,000 kids will be diagnosed with some form of cancer; thousands of others will face equally challenging diseases such as muscular dystrophy, diabetes, and others. Situations like the ones just described are only a sampling of the challenges these young survivors face. Not

What Causes Cancer?

No one really knows what causes cancer. It may be triggered by something in the environment or occur as a result of mutations or damage to a person's genes that the body is unable to repair. What we do know is what happens to the body when cancer strikes: cells of abnormal shape or size begin to grow and multiply out of control in the body. Sometimes, in a process called metastasis, cancer cells travel to other parts of the body, where they grow and replace normal tissue. As this happens, more and more of the body's nutrients are diverted to the cancerous tissue, leaving the rest of the body weak and vulnerable to illness and infection. Lymphoma, leukemia, brain cancer, and osteosarcoma are the cancers seen most frequently during childhood and the teen years.

only do these kids miss out on many of the milestones the rest of us take for granted, but they also experience isolation from their peers, frustration with staying on track with academics, the disruption of family relationships at home, and the anxiety and depression that accompany a serious, life-threatening disease like cancer. In a cruel, ironic twist, the very drugs that saved their lives may cause debilitating side effects and complications that add to the challenges they face.

What is so surprising though, is that almost without exception, the battles these young people fight leave them with a clarity of vision, purpose, and perspective that inspire those of us who, more than we realize, take so much of who we are and what we have for granted. Theirs is a message of hope, love, and yes, gratitude for their experiences. This message can teach us all.

Here are some of their stories.

Surviving Diabetes

Erika's Story, as told on the
Nemour Foundation's
TeensHealth Web site,
kidshealth.org

"You have juvenile diabetes." . . . Those were the words that changed my life forever. On August 31, 2000, I was lying in a hospital bed and the doctors were explaining that my pancreas had stopped functioning and I was no longer producing insulin. I was zoned out. Diabetes? How is that possible? Why me?. . .

FROM BEACH CHAIR TO HOSPITAL BED

During the summer of 2000 I was in Puerto Rico at a family reunion. We were relaxing by the beach when suddenly I had to go to the bathroom. Five minutes later I had to go again. I thought it was all the water I was drinking, so I cut back. Still, the frequent trips to the bathroom continued. When I had two "accidents," I realized that something was wrong. I mean, at age 12 these things don't happen. We called the doctor's office and they said it was probably just a urinary tract infection. I was given some antibiotics. Unfortunately, the medication had no effect. We cut our trip short and returned home. On the flight back, we had to ask for a seat close to the bathroom because my trips were increasing in frequency.

As soon as our plane landed, we headed to my physician's office. They took a urine sample, and for once I had no trouble giving one. When they tested it, they found traces of sugar in it. The physician then told me she wanted to check my blood sugar. I was scared! My grandparents have diabetes, so I knew that meant a needle. The machine read "466." My doctor stepped out of the room and, when she returned, she told me I had to go to the hospital. They were waiting for me there. She pulled my mom aside. I realized that things were not going well.

That's how I ended up with an IV in my arm, wearing one of those revealing robes; pulled from paradise into a world of white with beeping noises and bad food. During my time in the hospital, my family and I were taught about diabetes and how to manage it. I had to learn what to eat and how to give myself shots. I even had to improve my math skills in order to count carbohydrates.

I was overwhelmed! All I could think was, "I'm only 12 years old! How could this happen?" The fact that I was starting a new school that year didn't help. I didn't know how people would react or what they would say. What if they rejected me because of it? Would they make fun of me? Would I make friends? What if my blood sugar acted up and I made a fool of myself in class?

At first I was really quiet about having diabetes. I refused to tell anyone in school. Then, when my friends began asking me why I had to go to the nurse's office all the time, I decided to tell them. It turned out to be a good choice. Everyone was interested. They asked some funny questions like "Is it contagious?" (it's not) and "So, wait, you can never have sugar?" (I can). But I enjoyed explaining. When I had low blood sugar at school, my friends noticed it immediately and were able to help me.

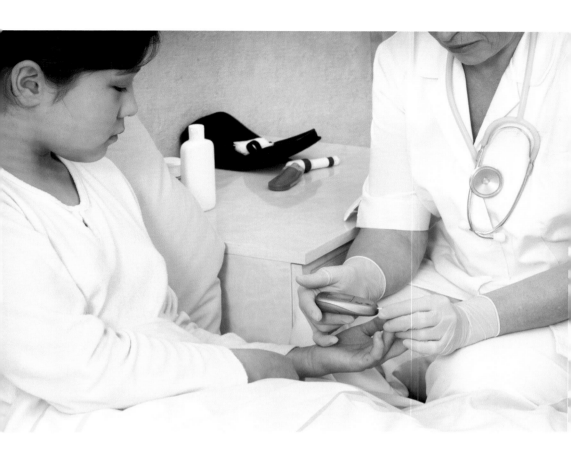

What is a day with diabetes like? I wake up and check my blood sugar using a finger-prick test. At breakfast I count carbohydrates and do some math in order to inject the proper dosage of insulin. At lunch, dinner, and before bed it's the same routine. If I have any symptoms of high or low blood sugar, then I have to prick my finger once again. It's not a good idea for me to skip meals. And I have to do extra checks on my blood sugar levels when I'm doing any kind of intense physical activity. Diabetes can also make someone moody. I will be happy and bouncing off the walls one second, and the next, I am yelling at my brothers.

Teens with diabetes must learn to monitor their blood-sugar levels. If blood sugar climbs too high, individuals may need to be hospitalized until their condition is stabilized.

I must confess that having diabetes has not been a walk in the park. There have been times when I want to rip my hair out! For example, I wasn't even able to go to a sleep-over until the tenth grade! My parents were kind of scared by it all.

I love sports. I can still play—I've played basketball, volleyball, and soccer—but I have to watch out for my blood sugar levels. During volleyball season, I tested my blood sugar more often. My blood sugar levels can affect my performance, so I wanted to make sure they were where they should be. Now I am getting in shape for soccer. All the running lowers my blood sugars, but the adrenaline rush can make them rise, causing my blood sugars to go up and down like a roller-coaster sometimes. . . .

My teenage years have been OK so far. I have learned how to handle my diabetes a lot better. In 2001, I got my insulin pump. That has completely changed my life, and things are a lot easier. I don't have to take a shot every time I eat, just one shot every 2 days. The pump takes a lot of the work off my hands. I still have to do calculations based on what I eat, but at least I don't have to give myself four shots a day. I only need to use a needle to insert a tiny plastic tube under my skin every 2 days. The pump is barely noticeable, too. Many people confuse it for a cell phone because of its size. It also comes with a lot of accessories, and as a girl, I love that!

I have also learned a lot more about diabetes and how to handle it. I have attended diabetes camps and have seen children much younger than I am with the same disease. Meeting them and their families has given me a more positive perspective on my diabetes. I have learned to whine less. If children 2 years of age can handle it, why can't I? I have also become involved with the American Diabetes Association and the Juvenile Diabetes Research Foundation. I want to help others with diabetes. I figure, "Hey, if I have to live with it, why not help others walking the same path?" If you help one person, you help the world.

LEARNING FOR LIFE

Diabetes has its ups and downs. Some days I think it's too much to handle, others I forget I even have it. I personally think diabetes has helped me grow as a person. I have become more responsible and mature. Because of my experience, I have decided to become a pediatric endocrinologist. This way I can help children with the same problems, and they can't tell me, "You don't know what I'm going through!" Diabetes has become a friend. All I have to do is view it as a part of me, not some disease. Yes, the road is hard, but nothing comes easy. You have to work for what you want.

Chapter Two
BRITTANY'S STORY

I grew up in a neighborhood full of tough, sports-playing boys and the only way I was going to fit in with them was if I could learn to keep up. So I did. I was out there every day playing kickball, football, baseball, anything. I absolutely love playing sports, and I am the type of girl who would rather play football in the mud than go shopping at the mall.

Before June of 2005 sports were what my life was about. I played soccer for school, a travel team, and was on both the indoor and outdoor track teams for my high school. I even made varsity track as an eighth-grader. I have always been the girl that none of the boys wanted to race in gym class for the simple reason that no boy wanted to "lose to a girl."

What Are Platelets?

Platelets are tiny cells floating in the blood that are shaped like disks or plates. They are produced in the bone marrow and their main function is to prevent bleeding by assisting with blood clotting. Chemotherapy can sometimes cause the number of platelets in a person's bloodstream to decrease.

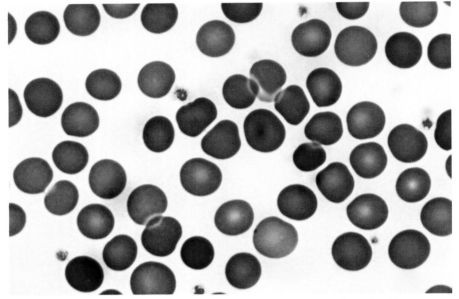

Platelets are the tiny cells in blood that cause your blood to clot if you are cut. Cancer treatment can interfere with normal platelet levels.

Then in June 2005 everything changed. I first noticed there was something wrong after running in a track meet. My knee didn't feel right. I went to see the athletic trainer and began physical therapy because we thought it was just a pulled muscle. It never crossed my mind that it could be cancer, and when the doctors told me that I had osteosarcoma, a bone cancer, my world fell apart.

The tumor was just above my right knee. Everything was a blur, and I never fully accepted or understood how much it was going to change my life. I was told that I would need chemotherapy, surgery, then even more chemotherapy, and that I would have to start right away. I wasn't even allowed to finish the school year.

All my treatments had to be done as an inpatient, so I spent most of my time at Golisano Children's Hospital at Strong Hospital in Rochester, New York, almost every weekend, usually going in on Fridays and leaving on Monday, only to come back again the following Friday.

I also had some unexpected hospital stays because of fevers and low blood counts. On December 23, 2004, my sixteenth birthday, I woke up with a fever and ended up in the hospital for six days getting blood and platelet transfusions. It was not my first choice of places to be on my "sweet 16," let alone Christmas, but everyone at the hospital, as

What Is Inpatient Treatment?

Inpatient treatment is when a person is admitted to a hospital for treatment and stays over at least one night. Outpatient treatment, on the other hand, is when a person is cared for at a doctor's office, clinic, or sometimes a hospital without staying overnight.

well as my family and best friend Charla, did a great job making sure it was still special for me.

One of the really good things about Golisano Children's Hospital is the people who work there: the nurses, doctors, and the **oncology** social worker Eric Iglewski. They became like family, and they were all absolutely wonderful, knowing exactly what to do or say to make my day a little brighter. Some of them were quite entertaining too. The only hard part about ending chemotherapy was saying good-bye to all of them.

I had limb-salvage surgery on August 30, 2005, the extent of which is still overwhelming to me. It's the hardest thing I had to deal with. I had a total knee replacement, and rods replaced part of my upper and lower leg. The recovery was hard; there are no words to fully describe the extreme pain. But the physical pain is easy compared to the emotional pain

oncology: is the study of the development, diagnosis, and treatment of cancerous tumors.

What Is Limb-Salvage Surgery?

Because Brittany's cancer had not spread to the nerves or blood vessels surrounding the bone in her leg, she was a candidate for limb-salvage surgery. In cases where these tissues have been invaded, amputation of the limb is recommended. Metal rods such as the ones placed in Brittany's leg are the material preferred by most doctors. Bone grafts from a bone bank carry greater risks, including a higher rate of fracture and infection.

that comes with the new rules I now have to live by for the rest of my life: no running or impact on my leg! For me this means my life will never be the same. No more track and no more soccer.

I was blindsided by this and took it harder than finding out that I had cancer. Right up to the moment before surgery, I prayed it was all a big mistake and I wouldn't need the surgery. I even threatened my parents with running away just to keep my knee so I could play soccer.

I have to fight back the tears every time I visit the track or soccer field. Sometimes it's

Chemotherapy is often administered intravenously. Drugs that kill cancer go directly into a vein.

What Does Chemotherapy Do?

In the case of cancer, chemotherapy is treatment with strong drugs that destroy quickly multiplying cancer cells, or make them less active. The drugs are usually given to the patient intravenously, meaning they are injected into a vein. They may also be given by injection into a muscle (intramuscular injection), injection just under the skin (subcutaneous injection), or by mouth in the form of pills (orally). Most drugs used to treat cancer also affect some healthy cells that divide rapidly, such as blood cells, hair and skin cells, and cells that line the digestive tract. When these cells are affected by the cancer drugs, the patient can experience side effects such as bruising or bleeding easily, loss of energy, loss of appetite, nausea, vomiting, hair loss, or mouth sores. For some patients, other medicines can be prescribed to help with these side effects. Chemotherapy is usually given in cycles, with alternating treatment and rest periods, so the patient has a chance to recover from the effects.

really hard and I have to turn back before I even get there. My coaches and teammates have all been very supportive. At first I tried to remain an active member of all my teams, but it was too hard to deal with, so I found a new way to remain active in sports; I am helping to coach a girl's travel soccer team for the local Soccer Association and I love every minute of it. Even though I cannot play, my love for soccer and track will never go away.

The good news is that after surgery the biopsy showed that the chemotherapy worked. One hundred percent of the cancer cells had been killed! The day I heard that, I knew everything would be okay. I am now in remission and get scans every three months to make sure the cancer has not returned. We celebrated my one-year-off-treatment anniversary in February with a party. It's almost like having two birthdays to celebrate. Every day, I thank God that I have my life back and get to do normal teenage stuff.

As hard as this has all been, many good things have come out of it. I have met so many amazing people and learned so much about myself and how precious life is. I will

What Is a Biopsy?

Biopsies are surgical procedures that are performed to diagnose and identify many different types of cancer. There are closed biopsies (performed with needles) and open biopsies, which are the type most commonly used in osteosarcoma patients. In this procedure the skin is opened, the tumor is actually exposed, and a portion of it is removed and examined under a microscope. Prior to a biopsy other imaging studies are usually performed such as MRIs (Magnetic Resonance Imaging) or CT (Computerized Tomography) to determine how far the cancer has spread and locate the exact area to be biopsied.

What Is Remission?

Someone is said to be in **remission** when his or her cancer responds to treatment or is brought under control. In complete remission all signs and symptoms of the disease disappear. If a cancer such as a tumor has shrunk but not disappeared completely it is referred to as a partial remission. Some cancers that have been in remission for a certain number of years are considered to be cured. Even if a cancer recurs after achieving remission, it may be brought under control again with further treatment.

never complain about a bad hair day again! I also connected with an organization called Teens Living with Cancer, which allows me to meet other teens with cancer. That has been very inspiring to me. I am lucky because my friends stayed by my side and supported me during my treatment, but no one can understand what I have been through like another teen with cancer can.

I have no idea what the future holds, but there is one thing I know for sure: I will make the best of every situation and live life to the fullest. I kicked cancer. I can do anything!

Brittany says, "I will make the best of every situation and live life to the fullest."

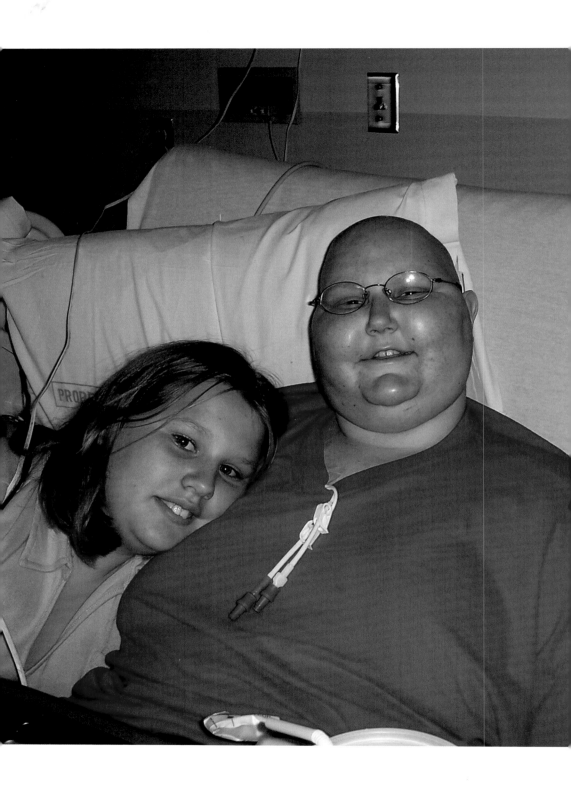

Chapter Three
BETHANY'S STORY

Hi. My name is Bethany. My date of birth is 5/10/89, my diagnosis is A.L.L., and my medical record number is 2273283. This is how I identify myself every time I go to the hospital. If I had met you two years ago I would have told you my name is Bethany and left it at that.

Cancer changes a person more than you'll ever know. Let me tell you a short story of a very long journey that I have been on while undergoing treatment for Acute Lymphoblastic Leukemia.

Two years ago I started to feel different. My step was slower and every day became harder to handle. I went to my doctor several times. She thought I had the flu. I am overweight, so I thought I was just getting heavier and that I

morphine:
is a powerful drug that is used to treat pain associated with cancer and other diseases. It is considered a narcotic, which is a type of drug that numbs the senses, relieves severe pain, and causes sleepiness.

oncologist:
is a doctor who specializes in diagnosing and treating cancer.

should really go on a diet and exercise more. Then I went back to the doctor, this time with crushing bone pain that ibuprofen and Tylenol wouldn't touch. I became weaker and weaker as they tried to figure out what was wrong. By the end of the day, the doctors in the small local hospital where I had been taken told me they suspected I had leukemia. That night I was hooked up to a *morphine* pump to help make me more comfortable. I could tell that my family was very scared. I don't think I would have been so frightened if I hadn't seen my mom crying. She is my security blanket and usually puts on a brave face no matter what we're up against. The doctor told me that the next day I would be transported to Strong Hospital in Rochester, New York. I should have gone that day but the weather was too stormy.

The next day, after I was settled into my new room at Strong, my primary **oncologist**, Dr. David Korones, came in to tell me that I had cancer. I asked if it was curable, and he said yes it was. I told him that I would eat kitty litter if it would help me to get better, and that it was time to get started! Little did I know what I was about to go through and how much my life as I knew it was about to change.

When I first lost my hair, I'll admit I was pretty devastated, but that lasted about a day. After that it became fun having no hair. Everyone thought that I was so cute. After my mom cut it she said, "Tweety! My baby!"

What Is Leukemia?

Leukemia is a cancer marked by an increase in the number of white blood cells called leukocytes. It is a cancer of the blood or blood-forming organs (bone marrow). Bone marrow is the spongy material in the cavities of the bones where blood is produced.

White blood cells

neutrophil eosinophil basophil monocyte lymphocyte

There are several different kinds of white blood cells, all of which contribute to the body's ability to defend itself against infection. Leukemia interferes with the body's normal production of white blood cells.

(She always thought I had looked like Tweety Bird when I was little because of my big eyes, long eyelashes, and the one or two strands of hair on my head—and now I looked like that again.) Being bald was also very convenient: I didn't have to wash my hair anymore. One of the best parts was scaring people as we drove by them in the car! No, I didn't care about the hair that much. I was more concerned about my health.

I have experienced a number of serious complications and side effects to medications over the past two years, including an anaphylactic allergic reaction to a chemotherapy drug, chemical hepatitis, the formation of three large blood clots in my heart, along with **pulmonary emboli**, kidney stones, **gastritis**, seven compression fractures in my spine which confined me to a wheelchair for a couple of months, and necrosis of the hip, which will require a total hip replacement. I gained forty pounds through steroid treatment and a drug called asparaginase—but don't worry: then I lost fifty pounds after throwing up almost nonstop for three straight months.

Even during my worst times though, I have truly seen cancer as a blessing. The

What Is an Anaphylactic Allergic Reaction?

Anaphylaxis is a very serious and sudden allergic reaction involving a person's whole body. A trigger—in Bethany's case the chemotherapy drug—causes large of amounts of different substances, including one called histamine, to be released into the bloodstream. This in turn leads to any number of possible physical reactions, some of them life-threatening: itching, sneezing, difficulty breathing, rapid heartbeat, cardiac arrest, nausea, cramps, vomiting, bloating, diarrhea, and more.

When the Treatment Makes You Sick

Bethany developed three large blood clots in her heart as a result of a side effect of one of her chemotherapy drugs. Along with this side effect, her body perceived the catheter placed near her heart as a foreign object which caused clots to surround the catheter as it attempted to remove it from the body (an immune reaction). Bethany's catheter was made of soft plastic. It was surgically placed in her neck vein where it led to the opening of her heart. Intravenous chemotherapy and other medications are administered through a catheter, and blood is regularly withdrawn from it for testing. Because her clots could not be surgically removed without serious risk, Bethany was given heparin shots in the thigh or stomach twice a day to reduce her blood's ability to clot. This allowed the clots to slowly dissolve and flatten against the wall of her heart.

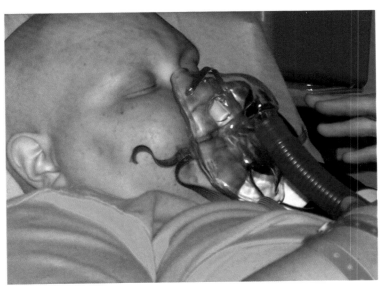

Bethany receiving oxygen during one of her treatment's many complications.

What Is Necrosis?

Necrosis or osteonecrosis is a medical term referring to the breakdown of bone cells. Many kids who are on protocols that include high-dose corticosteroids develop osteonecrosis of bone tissue. Experts believe this may occur because steroids interfere with the body's ability to break down fatty substances, which clog and narrow the blood vessels. This, in turn, reduces the amount of blood flow to the bone. When this happens in areas such as the hip, pain can be excruciating and difficult to tolerate. Narcotics such as morphine may be prescribed to control this pain along with NSAIDs (nonsteroidal anti-inflammatory drugs).

most important reason I believe this to be true is that I have met so many wonderful people. The nurses, doctors, and social workers who spend their days in a hospital are a special breed of people and are simply amazing. I know I can trust the doctors on my hematology-oncology team because they are so honest, caring, and compassionate. One of the things I like best about them is that they expect me to ask questions and make suggestions about my own treatment, and they want to know what I'm thinking and feeling. Eric Iglewski, the social worker for hematology/oncology, is such a cool guy. He is the most in-tune man I have ever met. Eric listens to you as though you are the only thing that matters at that moment in time, and what you say is golden. He knows when to give me space and when to act goofy like a best friend. And of course there are the nurses. They are so genuinely nice that you simply cannot get mad at them, no matter how much you want to scream and yell at someone for the way your life is going.

Because the people on the inpatient adolescent unit have seen so many other kids going through the same treatment as me, they were able to encourage me and give me hope and strength to believe I could come out the other side strong and well. And people *really* looked at me strangely when I told

Bethany with her nurses.

Some people develop chemical hepatitis (inflammation of the liver) as a result of the toxic nature of their chemotherapy drugs, especially during the second phase in some treatments called intensification. Hepatitis can cause jaundice, a yellowing of the skin, eyes, and body fluids.

them I actually looked forward to my lumbar punctures. The nurse practitioner who performed mine has a great sense of humor, always made sure I was completely relaxed and comfortable before we started, and let me bring my CDs for our listening pleasure! She got a kick out of the fact that I enjoy a lot of the oldies she grew up with!

These people have become what I know will be lifelong friends and sort of . . . well . . . family. I can tell them anything and feel so comfortable around them. I look forward to giving them what they call my "Bethy hugs." And then there is my Joann. All of the nurse practitioners are wonderful, but Joann, she's "mine." We have so much in common and we formed an instant bond from the moment we met. We both enjoy PBS and the great outdoors, and we treat our pets like humans.

About six months into my treatment when I began experiencing some pretty scary complications, I was introduced to a wonderful therapist named Patty. I didn't know when

What Causes Compression Fractures?

Compression fractures occur in the back when the bones of the spine—the vertebrae—break or crack due to being squished or compressed. These fractures can be caused by injury, such as falling or being in a car accident; by osteoporosis, a condition in which bones become fragile and break easily; or by cancerous tumors that eat away at or weaken the bones.

Why Do Cancer Patients Take Steroids?

Steroids are hormonal substances made naturally by the body, but they can also be produced artificially and used as drugs. Steroids can help cancer patients in a number of ways: They can help prevent sickness caused by chemotherapy; increase the effectiveness of chemotherapy; and reduce swelling in tissues around a tumor. Some of the side effects of steroids are actually beneficial to patients with advanced cancer. Steroids can cause an increase in both appetite and energy level; these effects help cancer patients who have lost their appetite and strength to gain weight and feel better.

we met that Patty would have such a great impact on my life. She has helped me meet many challenges and gotten me through some pretty horrible times. I tell Patty everything, and I keep no secrets from her.

Another very courageous and special person I have met along the way is Lauren Spiker who started the Teens Living with Cancer organization after her own daughter lost her battle with a rare form of leukemia. This organization has given me many opportunities to meet other teens struggling with cancer, and Lauren has become a dear friend.

And I've become acquainted with people from almost every specialty along the way: cardiology, nephrology, urology, gastroenterology, and orthopedics. All I see when I think of my healers are smiles. Spending time in a hospital has made me realize how many

What Is a Lumbar Puncture?

An intrathecal or lumbar puncture is chemotherapy that is injected into the cerebrospinal fluid of the spinal column. This is a standard part of treatment for many types of leukemia that is performed periodically throughout a patient's protocol. A long (usually around 12 inches!) hollow needle is inserted into the spinal column between the lumbar vertebrae of the spine where spinal fluid is first drawn off for examination to be sure cancerous cells are not present. Chemotherapy is then injected to prevent cancer from developing in the spinal cord and brain. Conventional chemotherapy that enters the bloodstream through a catheter would not be able to cross the blood brain barrier. This treatment was developed after it was discovered that leukemia could travel to the central nervous system after being eradicated from the rest of the body.

wonderful people there are out there who are devoted to helping others.

Another reason I feel cancer has been a blessing is that I have developed a relationship with my mother and the rest of my family that I might not have otherwise. A mother is more than just the person who gave birth to you, I've discovered; at least in my case, she is comfort and love. I never knew that a mother's touch could be healing until I got cancer. It's as if there is a flow of electric energy from her body into mine, making me better. I remember lying in my hospital bed while she would sit beside me stroking my brow trying to get the crinkled ridge in the middle to relax. Without her, I wouldn't be here now. I'm certain of it. I cannot count how many questions she has asked my doctors over the past two years. I consider her to be the most important part of my treatment protocol. She has learned to do things like give me shots, IV fluids, draw my labs, and change my dressings. She has stayed with me during every hospital admission and even quit her job to stay home with me. My mom always says that any mother would have, but I don't believe it. There are many children in the hospital without their moms. I cannot imagine that. She has not left my side for more than a few hours at a time since my diagnosis. My mother and I have a relationship where I can tell her anything and she can tell me anything. We cry about

protocol: is a carefully constructed treatment plan that has been designed after clinical trials determine the most effective method of administering drugs along with appropriate dosage and when they should be given.

Bethany with her sister Abigail.

the smallest things and laugh so hard at the silliest things.

My sister and I have also come to realize how important we are to each other. Even though she is five years younger than me, at times she takes care of me as though she were the big sister. She always makes sure that I'm okay and takes care of me when I need help. And my dad always seems to keep the humor going when I need it. He helps keep the whole family sane. He and my sister made a very frightening dash back home from a school trip to New York City when the doctors discovered the blood clots in my heart, and we weren't sure what was going to happen. I hope to make it up to my sister by taking a long family trip together when this is all over.

I've learned so much these past two years. I've learned that my family, love, and reaching out to others are the most important things to me. Without them there is no true happiness. Cancer has helped me grow up into the person I've always wanted to be, decide what I believe in, and determine what I want out of life. This illness has made me think about the way the world works and how interconnected everything is. I learned how much the world takes for granted too. Simple things like taking a shower, brushing my teeth, and walking up the stairs are amazing luxuries and require a lot more strength than you think. Every day I wake up, I am thankful that I'm alive!

Bethany today.

To anyone just starting out on this journey I would tell you to remember: you know your mind and your body better than anyone. Always tell people how you feel, and don't be afraid to ask for help when you need it, because there are terrific people in this world who are willing to help!

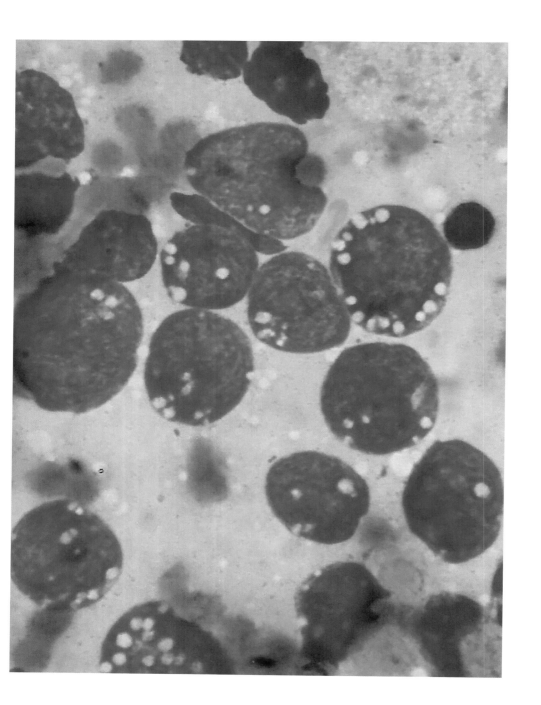

Chapter Four

ABIJAH'S STORY

A bijah was a senior enjoying his last year in high school, playing basketball and eagerly awaiting the chance to go away to college. He'd grown up on a family farm, had always worked hard, and had always been, as the saying goes "healthy as a horse." In his entire school career he had not missed one day of school. Every year he earned an award for perfect attendance, and there was no reason to expect he would not receive one for his thirteenth year running. He had constructed a careful roadmap for his future; as the first person in his family to graduate high school and attend college, he planned to acquire double majors in biology and chemistry along with a certification in secondary education.

A diagnosis of lymphoblastic lymphoma derailed those plans and turned Abijah's life upside down. Widely admired and respected because of his hard work and easygoing nature, Abijah was a great favorite among his peers and teachers. News of his illness rippled through his community, sending everyone into a tailspin. They had never doubted the advantages of living in a small town, but now Abijah and his family discovered firsthand how generous and supportive everyone could be. His school, area churches, and other local organizations organized fundraisers and dinners to help with the cost of treatment and associated expenses like travel and meals. Neighbors and family pitched in to help with the farm work while his mom, dad, and sister spent time with him in the hospital. Unfortunately, the news Abijah received upon his initial diagnosis was not encouraging.

Because Abijah was eighteen, he had the choice of being seen by a doctor who specialized in adult oncology or by a pediatric

What Is Lymphoma?

The lymphatic system is made up of a network of tiny vessels filled with clear fluid called lymph which contains infection-fighting white blood cells called lymphocytes. Lymph nodes, or what are referred to as glands, are also a part of the lymphatic system. Cancer of the lymphatic system is called lymphoma, of which there are two types: Hodgkin's disease and non-Hodgkin's lymphoma.

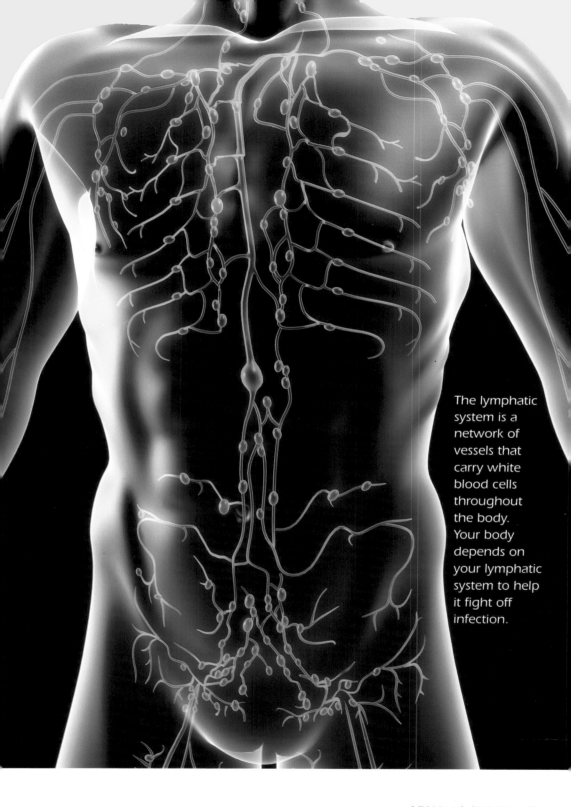

The lymphatic
system is a
network of
vessels that
carry white
blood cells
throughout
the body.
Your body
depends on
your lymphatic
system to help
it fight off
infection.

What Are Cancer Stages?

Staging is the process of determining how advanced a cancer is at the time of diagnosis. There are four stages of cancer, which are assigned a Roman number anywhere from I (1) to IV (4), with IV considered to be the most serious or advanced stage. Three things are usually taken into consideration when arriving at a number including tumor size, how many lymph nodes have been affected in the area surrounding the tumor, and whether the cancer has spread or metastasized to other organs of the body.

pediatrics: is the branch of medicine concerned with the development and health of infants, children, and adolescents.

oncologist. His first visit was with a doctor in adult oncology. His hopes were dashed when he was told very matter-of-factly that his cancer was stage IV, the most advanced stage; he would not graduate high school and would not be attending college. Reeling from the shock, Abijah and his family regrouped and considered their options. They decided to seek treatment in **pediatrics** where cure rates are higher, and philosophies and approaches are more intimate and caring. Abijah's new doctor told him that even though it would be tough going, there was every reason to hope.

This began a journey of ups and downs that would span two years. Abijah experienced all the usual reactions to treatment: nausea, vomiting, weakness, and hair loss. In addition, high doses of steroids and a drug with particularly nasty side effects called L-asparaginase caused wild fluctuations in weight, edema, and short-term diabetes. His glucose levels reached as high as 600, and it was not uncommon for him to lose ten pounds overnight from huge outputs of urine as his body ate away at his muscle.

As his high school graduation approached, it became obvious that Abijah would need to remain in the hospital due to the severe spinal headaches he was experiencing. He would miss the moment so many of us look forward to with such anticipation; he would not be forgotten by his classmates, however. In a symbol of their solidarity and support for their good friend, several of Abijah's friends showed up for graduation with shaven heads; when the audience saw them, they burst into cheers and applause. Days later, a private graduation ceremony was held in the hospital. In full cap and gown, Abijah was presented with his diploma from the high school principal and superintendent as family, friends, doctors, and nurses looked on.

Though still receiving intensive chemotherapy, Abijah continued to look ahead, refusing to give up his plans to attend SUNY Geneseo, his initial college of choice. After missing only one semester, he enrolled as a full-time student. Abijah's girlfriend Heather remained steadfastly by his side, despite his willingness to grant her the freedom to enjoy her own high school experience. Almost two years later, an end was in sight as Abijah approached the final few weeks of his

edema: *is excessive swelling or accumulation of fluid in body tissues.*

treatment—but not without one more scare that nearly took his life.

One night shortly after his mother flushed his catheter, Abijah sat at his computer working on a school assignment. He began to feel a little chilled and decided he was probably coming down with a cold or some other virus. The following morning he continued to feel unwell, so his mother drove him to his college class. Before long he had spiked a fever and was shivering uncontrollably. Realizing there was something seriously wrong his parents rushed him to the hospital emergency room.

The staff, who are used to unsettling situations, remained calm, thinking that he was suffering from some ordinary bug. The nurse assigned to Abijah left to get him a blanket. By now, Abijah had begun to vomit and his shivering became so severe his father actually had to hold him down on the bed.

The fear and stress of the moment caused Abijah's mother to pass out on the floor. His father yelled for help, and several nurses rushed to the room and surrounded his mother. As she came to, she shouted, "Never mind me, help Abijah!"

It soon became clear that what Abijah was suffering from was something called septicemia or sepsis, which can occur when an infection from one site of the body enters the bloodstream. It is especially common in cancer patients undergoing chemotherapy

What Is a Catheter?

Catheters are thin tubes, usually made of soft, flexible silicone, that administer medicine directly to a patient's bloodstream. They require diligent care, which includes daily flushing of the "line" with saline and infusing it with a small amount of a mixture of antibiotic and heparin. This helps prevent infection as well as clot formation near the line. The site where the line exits the body needs to be kept very clean, and dressings are changed twice a week. Patient and family members are instructed on how to care for the catheter with sterile dressing kits that include antiseptic swabs, sterile gloves, and face masks to prevent contamination of the site.

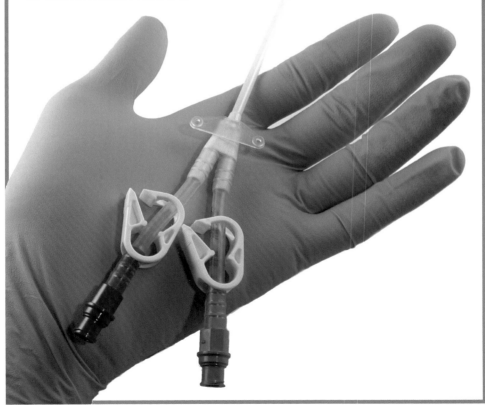

whose white blood cells have been suppressed, which lowers the body's ability to fight infection. As the family recalled the activities of the previous day, they realized that Abijah had begun to feel unwell shortly after having his central line flushed. Apparently, bacteria residing someplace in the catheter was flushed directly into the bloodstream near his heart, making him dangerously ill.

Abijah was admitted to the hospital and received strong antibiotics to combat the infection raging in his body. He passed in and out of consciousness and suffered wild hallucinations. After a day or so he began to improve and awoke to find his mom seated next to him in the hospital. A decision was made to have his catheter removed, and he would have his few remaining treatments through a traditional IV line.

Abijah is now twenty-two years old. He has been in remission for almost two years, has completed most of his education and will soon be student teaching. He and Heather are engaged and plan to marry when he has secured a job and can settle down. Like many people who have had cancer, he feels the good times have outweighed the bad; he has definitely learned a lot about himself and the world around him. He chooses to view his experience in a positive light, taking what he has learned and using it in a peer mentoring group to help other kids who have been

hallucinations: *are sensory experiences that seem real to the person who is having them, but that are not actually happening. The person sees, hears, tastes, smells, or touches something that isn't really there.*

diagnosed with cancer, as well as educating classmates about cancer at the request of his college professors. He finds he focuses more on what he wants to do with his life, knowing firsthand that the time we all have here may be shorter than we think.

Chapter Five
MIKE'S STORY

You sense something special about Mike the first moment you see him—and it's not just his dashing good looks, wide smile, or the mischievous gleam in his eye. He walks confidently, though with a bit of a limp. With the humor and frankness that are so characteristic of him, he lifts up his pant leg and raps his artificial leg. The fact that he does this astride a revving snowmobile is no less surprising. The image pretty much defines Mike: all go, without much stop!

Mike developed a love of things on wheels at an early age. As a young teen, he raced dirt bikes until a broken vertebra put him in a back brace. His doctor warned him that racing his bike again could paralyze him from the waist down. He complied with his doctors wishes, sold his dirt bike—and bought an all-terrain vehicle! It was a little bit safer at least and

A relapse is when a disease returns after a period of improvement.

still satisfied his love for racing. He never sustained any serious injuries on the ATV beyond a few bumps and scrapes.

One day, however, he noticed that what he had believed was just a bruise had begun to swell. In a very short time it was the size of a golf ball and so painful he wasn't able to kick start his ATV. His dad noticed he wasn't riding and asked him why. When he saw Mike's leg, he immediately took him to see the doctor.

X-rays revealed that half of Mike's tibia was missing. Just before Christmas, when Mike was eighteen, a bone biopsy confirmed a diagnosis of osteosarcoma. Not much of a Christmas present!

After New Year's, Mike began four months of chemotherapy. Eventually, he underwent

What Is Osteosarcoma?

Osteosarcoma is a form of bone cancer that affects boys more often than girls, and usually occurs during a growth spurt. Experts speculate that the rapid rate at which cells reproduce during this time may have something to do with the tendency for errors to occur in the process. Some believe a certain growth factor present in the body may contribute to the development of osteosarcoma. This theory has given rise to research into ways to slow these growth factors. The long bones of the body are the ones most likely to be affected. These include the bones above and below the knee and between the elbow and shoulder. Persistent pain that is not associated with exercise and swelling in a specific area of these bones are signs of osteosarcoma.

total knee replacement, and half of his tibia was replaced as well. These surgeries were followed by six more months of chemotherapy. He remembers that at the time, he advised the doctors to go ahead and take the whole leg because he knew his cancer would come back. Unfortunately, his instincts proved to be correct. In six months, his cancer had relapsed. This meant several more months of treatment before his leg could be amputated and five more months of treatment after surgery.

> ## What Is a Tibia?
>
> The tibia is the inner and larger of the two leg bones extending from the knee to the ankle. It is also known as the shinbone.

Going through such a grueling ordeal would understandably devastate anyone, not to mention a young man entering the prime of life. But although Mike definitely experienced a period of physical and emotional adjustment to the drastic changes in his life, he remained undaunted and continued to embrace life with all the enthusiasm and vigor he always had. In no time he was racing again, this time on snowmobiles.

While riding his snowmobile, he was thrown from his machine and was sent toppling downhill. Rushing to his side, friends asked if he was all right. He grinned and pointed to his missing leg: "Yeah, I'm okay, but I can't feel my leg!" In his adrenalin-filled state, he wasn't aware of too much pain until the next day—when his medical team discovered he had shattered the end

Mike's sense of humor played an important role in his ability to cope with cancer.

What Is Chemotherapy?

Chemotherapy refers to drugs or chemical agents that are given to destroy cancer cells. An initial course of chemotherapy is administered to shrink and contain the tumor, after which surgery is performed to remove it. This is followed by more chemotherapy to be certain that any remaining cancer cells are destroyed to prevent them from traveling to other parts of the body. For someone like Mike who has been diagnosed with an isolated tumor, surgery is used in combination with chemotherapy.

of his "stump." Four more inches had to be removed from his leg.

Mike admits that his lifestyle leaves many shaking their heads. "Needless to say, you would think I would stay off of snowmobiles, but you would be wrong. I still ride to this very day. It just proves what the human body is capable of. You can do anything if you try hard enough. Just think—I once was in your shoes. Now I'm only in one shoe, and I'm doing great!"

Because of cancer, Mike says, "I look at life in a totally different way. I'm a lot more outgoing." He also says the two biggest things he has learned are to "live life to the fullest and treat every day like it could be your last," and also that "there is nothing you can't do if you push yourself . . . and you will learn so much about yourself in the process." What bothers him the most is that many people tend to feel sorry for him or look at him as if he were handicapped, but they soon find out

Mike's words
of wisdom:
"Never give up
because there is
always light at
the end of the
tunnel."

that "I have more ability than most people, even though I have lost a leg."

Maintaining his sense of humor and having the ability to laugh at himself also keeps him centered. And he isn't above pulling pranks like the one he shares about shooting a game of pool with some buddies. A few girls were in the pool hall who Mike hadn't met. Recognizing an opportunity to have some fun, he inserted his stump into a pocket of the pool table and began pulling on it, shouting, "Somebody give me a hand, my leg is stuck!" As he predicted the girls rushed to his aid, only to erupt in shrieks and then laughter when his stump was dislodged from the pocket.

Mike admits that having cancer has resulted in the loss of some friends. "You learn who your real friends are, but I have made so many new friends along the way. The people going through the stuff you've gone through are so real compared to the people who haven't had cancer." Mike is involved with a group of teen cancer survivors, and he offers encouragement and support to those who need it. His warmth, openness, and sincerity win over young and old alike, whether male or female.

His advice to those newly diagnosed: "Never give up because there is always light at the end of the tunnel." He cautions the rest of us who may think it can never happen to us to remember that cancer does not discriminate. "It doesn't care what your age, color, or gender is."

Chapter Six
TOREY'S STORY

Torey is living proof that good things come in small packages. A petite brunette whose soft brown eyes seem to take up most of her face, she appears almost frail. After being with her for just a short time, though, you'll realize she is a person of great stature indeed.

In 1997, at the age of fourteen, Torey was diagnosed with stage-IV **neuroblastoma**, a rare form of cancer that accounts for only 7 percent of the cancers diagnosed in children. Unfortunately, she is included in an even more rare subset; only 3 percent of those with neuroblastoma are over the age of ten.

In the first year alone of Torey's diagnosis, she endured chemotherapy, spot and total body radiation, two bone marrow transplants, and two surgeries. These treatments helped her achieve remission by the spring of 1998.

neuro-blastoma: starts out as a solid tumor made up of immature or developing nerve cells that may originate in the adrenal glands, the abdomen, or in nerve tissue of the chest, neck, or pelvis. Stage IV is the most advanced stage, meaning it has spread from its original site to other areas of the body.

What Is Radiation Therapy?

The use of high energy X-rays to destroy cancerous cells or shrink tumors is called radiation therapy. Sometimes this is accomplished by placing radioactive material inside a tumor (internal radiation). It may also be performed on the external surfaces of the body (external beam radiation therapy). This type of treatment is usually administered on an outpatient basis in a clinic. Depending on what kind of cancer is being treated, radiation may be used alone or in combination with surgery and chemotherapy. Bethany and Kim received radiation to the brain to prevent their leukemia from traveling to the central nervous system. In order to be certain their radiation was directed to a very precise area of the brain, they were first fitted with a rigid, plastic mask with openings for their eyes, nose, and mouth. During each treatment the mask was attached to the table where they received their treatments to ensure they would remain in the exact same position. Meditation, relaxation techniques, and listening to music are all good ways to deal with the anxiety that often accompanies radiation treatments.

Though she was by no means worry-free, she remained cancer-free the next few years and was able to graduate high school in 2001.

Torey entered college in the fall of 2001, but by her sophomore year in 2002, she began to suspect that something was not quite right. She was experiencing feelings of heaviness in her legs and other signs of

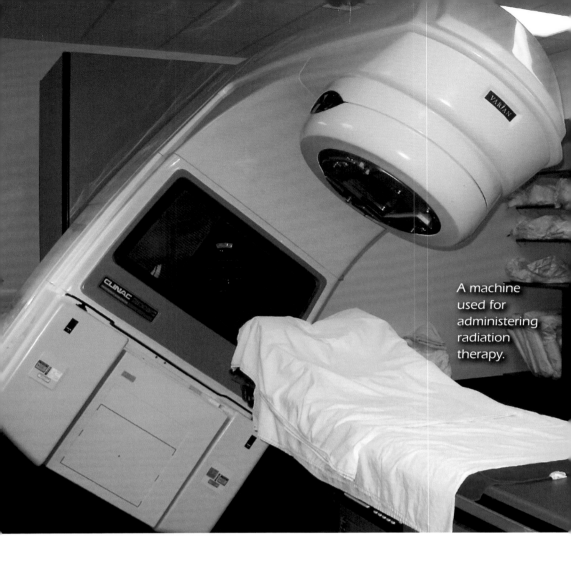

A machine used for administering radiation therapy.

weakness. Scans performed in the summer after her sophomore year showed that her cancer was active again, although it was not growing fast. She was sent to Sloan-Kettering Memorial Cancer Center in New York City, where she would undergo a six-hour surgery to remove every visible sign of cancer. Afterward, she returned home to have spot radiation at Strong Hospital in Rochester, which

renal failure: is when the kidneys stop working.

dialysis: a patient is hooked up to a machine that filters the blood and eliminates the waste for him or her.

nephrostomy bag: is used to collect urine from a plastic tube—or catheter—that has been inserted through the skin and into the kidney to drain it.

meant that she had reached her body's limit of allowable radiation.

But the news was good: another remission! Torey returned to college in August of 2003 to start her junior year, but by the following summer she was readmitted to the hospital with complete **renal failure**. Her cancer was back and growing aggressively. She had to undergo **dialysis** for a time, but luckily her kidneys jumpstarted themselves and began functioning again. Unfortunately, her cancer had spread, infiltrating both ureters, which are the tubes that empty urine from the kidneys into the bladder. This meant she had to have catheters placed in both kidneys to drain her urine into **nephrostomy bag**s.

Torey felt like she was imprisoned by her body. She told her doctors, "I would rather die than continue living this way." One of her kidneys had sustained a great deal of damage, so she decided to have surgery, not knowing if it would still be there when she woke up after the operation. Luckily, her left kidney was found to be functioning at 9 percent of normal function and her right kidney at 91 percent; this meant she could keep them both! She began chemotherapy once again, and by February of 2006, she had no active signs of cancer. In August of 2006 she started her senior year of college, and in the spring of 2007 she completed her chemotherapy.

Eleven years after her initial diagnosis, she remains cancer free, has graduated college,

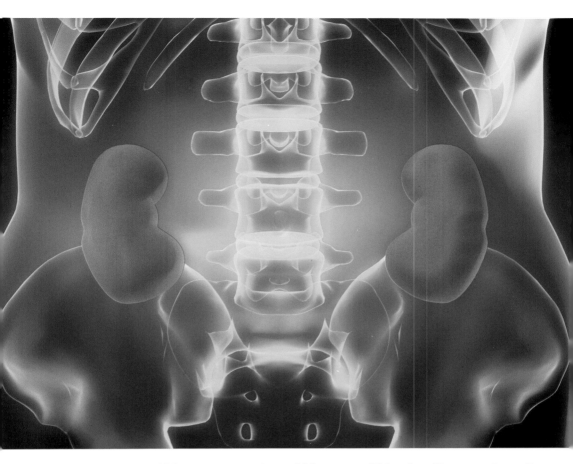

Every day, your kidneys process about 200 quarts of blood to filter out about 2 quarts of waste products and extra water. The waste and extra water become urine, which flow to your bladder through tubes called ureters. Without your kidneys, the waste products would stay in your body and eventually poison you. That is why Torey's kidney function was so important to her survival.

and secured a teaching position in Washington, D.C. Her strength, courage, and perseverance are awe-inspiring, especially to her fellow cancer survivors who know all too well the significance of what she has been through.

Chapter Seven

TALKING WITH CANCER SURVIVORS: FINDING A NEW NORMAL

Recently, Torey, Abijah, Kim (who was diagnosed with a high-risk leukemia), and Bethany met to talk and share some of their experiences. When a group of young people like these come together, the atmosphere is an unusual combination of excitement at the chance they have to connect about things the rest of us can't begin to imagine, and relief that they are able to let down their guard and discuss topics that can make other people uncomfortable. Conversation is quick and lively with comments overlapping as they eagerly respond to one another; they're so grateful to have their own feelings and insights validated by someone else who "gets it." As Brittany said, "No one can understand what I have been through like another teen with cancer can."

The young people were willing to share the stories. They also answered a few questions.

Do you feel there are stereotypes about people with cancer?

Kim: Yes, I think there are. When most people hear the word cancer, I think they picture someone who is bald, pale, and swollen!

Bethany: And people really need to be educated more about cancer and the fact that there are different kinds, different treatments, with different cure rates and chances of survival. This is even true of people who have cancer themselves. I remember one time a lady who had had breast cancer came up to me and told me not to worry, that treatment would get so much easier. I know she was trying to be nice, and I know breast cancer is pretty scary too, but something like leukemia that is spread throughout your entire body means that your treatments are every week for two years. They just keep slamming your body over and over to get rid of it. It can get pretty hard on all your organs too. With some other types of cancer they do surgery, you have some rounds of chemo, and maybe radiation, and you're done.

Are these stereotypes a form of prejudice?

Bethany: They can be. I think a lot of people hear the word cancer and they feel sorry for you and just assume that you're going to die. People are also afraid of getting close to you—I think that even though they know it isn't contagious, there are still some superstitious feelings out there that you might catch it.

Torey: I remember one day when my neighbor's little boy, who was around six years old at the time, asked me if he could have a sip of my McDonald's drink. He wanted to know if he could catch what I had and I said, "No, it's not contagious." His mother yelled at him, but I told her it was okay, he had to know.

How did having cancer change how people looked at you or interacted with you? Did it change the way other kids acted around you? Did you lose friends or make new friends?

Torey: When I was first diagnosed everybody smiled at me and acted like I was their friend. It was funny because when the educational liaison came to school to talk about my cancer my enemies from middle school cried the hardest. I'm not sure if they felt guilty or just wanted the attention. They were all nicer to me for a while, but their true colors came through again later on. I lost my best friend after my bone marrow transplant. It became pretty obvious after a while that she was coming to my house just because I lived in town and it was convenient for her because she could hang out other places using my house as a base. My mom finally confronted her about it. It was pretty hard for me because at that time in your life your friends can feel more important to you than your family. But I've made new friends who have listened to me and tried to understand what I'm going through.

Abijah: It was kind of interesting for me because people that I expected would come to see me in the hospital didn't, and people I never expected would, did. It really showed me who cared. But it's hard to be upset with anybody over it. Most of my friends were in the middle of baseball season in our senior year and there was a lot going on. Some of my older friends who were in college were home for the summer and they came up to see me, so that was nice.

Bethany: At first my friends came to see me and called all the time. When I came home from my first hospital admission they had a Valentine's Day party for me and brought me a gigantic white teddy bear. As time went on though, I developed more and more complications. I swelled up like a balloon. My face was so swollen I could hardly see over my cheeks, and my ankles were so stiff and huge my parents used to have to place my feet on the running board of our SUV so I could get in it. The only place I went was to the hospital for my treatments. People stopped calling so much, and obviously I couldn't go anywhere with them so I think they just got out of the habit of asking. Once you're out of the loop for a while you feel like an outsider and it's really hard to find your way back inside when you've missed so much. I think they were really afraid I was going to die too, and they just didn't know what to say.

Kim: I was in my senior year of college when I was diagnosed. Every year during my college breaks I would go home and get together with some of my friends from high school. Each year fewer and fewer people would end up coming to our gatherings. When I came home from college during Thanksgiving break the first year of my treatment, I decided to have some friends over—tons of people showed up. It kind of bugged me. I always wondered if they just came to say goodbye because they thought I was going to die. I did have a few friends who really stuck by me through the whole ordeal though.

What did you learn from cancer? How has it changed who you are?

Abijah: I think it focused me more on what I wanted to do with my life because I knew my life might be shorter.

Bethany: Before I got cancer, all I could think about was having fun and who was going to have the next party. Life was moving really fast and I wasn't paying much attention to my grades. I really didn't like the person I was becoming. When I got cancer that all changed. I realized how important my family was to me and how heavily I relied on them. And I still do!

Torey: After treatment, life doesn't just pick up where it left off. It's not a fairy tale. Things don't magically go back to the way they were. But instead I have had to make a new normal. I think cancer has really helped me find out the meaning of life.

Kim: My priorities changed for sure. I was too concerned about materialistic things. Cancer woke me up. I found out who I was. And I found out things *can happen* and we're not indestructible. Anyone can get cancer. I try to remember that every day could be my last. In some ways I feel more mature than my friends because of my experiences, but I know I'm behind

Cancer taught Kim important lessons. "Cancer woke me up," she said. "I found out who I was."

in other ways. Most of my friends have graduated from college and are getting married.

Bethany: One of the things I've learned—that I really wish I hadn't had to—is what it feels like to get old. Because of the compression fractures in my spine and my hip collapse, I've had to use a wheelchair, crutches, a commode, and a special chair for the shower. It's awful to be so weak you have to spend most of your day worrying about how you're going to get from point A to point B and whether the places you may need to go have handrails and sturdy steps. My heart breaks for old people when I see them toddling along because I think I know how they feel having to depend on everyone else around them.

What is the worst thing about having cancer?

Torey: For me, the worst thing about having cancer is that even while you are in a crowded room, you can feel all alone. Even at Camp Good Days, which is a camp for kids with cancer, I can feel all alone. I am constantly reaching out online to find someone who has been through what I have (neuroblastoma)—battling something that is chronic. At one point I started visiting kids in the bone marrow transplant unit of the hospital, but every time I got close to somebody, they would die! A couple of years ago I started doing Novenas. My cancer went away—was it the prayers, or was it the chemo? I'm at peace with God right now. If my cancer comes back, will I doubt my faith? I don't know.

Kim: For me the worst thing about having cancer is the way time just stands still. This three-week cycle just keeps repeating over and over: recover from treatment, go back to treatment—you're just stuck in these cycles of chemotherapy over and over—everything is the same for you, and everyone else is moving forward. I had no self-confidence while I was bald and puffy from steroids. I didn't want to see people. And I was so tired! Have you ever been that tired in your life? Can you imagine ever being that tired again?

Bethany: Oh, I know! I didn't even want to talk—at times I couldn't even sit up. I was that tired! I was in a mental fog and felt like I was living life in a tunnel. I remember when I was at my sickest after they found the blood clots in my heart I had kind of a meltdown in the hospital. I started to cry and told my mom and one of the nurses about how I was sick of death and dying, sick of hearing about wars and kids starving. I really scared the nurses. They brought a psychologist in to talk to me who said they could pre-scribe some kind of anti-anxiety pills for me, but I didn't want them. I guess being so sick just made things seem so clear to me, and I wondered why we have to bring on so much senseless suffering and pain when things like cancer can come along for no reason and cause pain, suf-fering, and death? Why can't we choose not to do things that hurt us? Why can't we choose to get along? We have a choice about so many things when compared with the things we have no control over like cancer. Why do people have to be so angry when we have such a short time on this earth? Why can't we try to be happy? We are capable of so many things. I never told my mom this until I was done with my treatments, but sometimes when I was so tired and so depressed I would look at my pill basket in the next room and think about all the medication in there—my mind would play tricks on me, and some-times I didn't know if I could trust myself not to go in there and take a bunch of it. I never wanted to be alone for very long.

Does having cancer change your ideas about what is important—and what things are really worth getting upset over or griping about?

Bethany: It's kind of hard to listen to somebody complain about a bad hair day or a broken fingernail when you've been through what we've been through. A while ago one of my friends couldn't drive when she had to go on a certain medication. She was ticked because she couldn't go places and she felt so confined. I wanted to ask her: "How do you think I've been feeling the last three years?"

Abijah: I feel about 50/50 when it comes to telling people to stop complaining. If they are whining about something that is really not a big deal, I will say something. This person started to talk about how much pain he was in and stopped himself by saying, "Oh, sorry Abijah! I know I shouldn't complain when my situation can't compare to yours." But everybody has the right to complain. If it is the worst pain you've ever felt, you're entitled to those feelings. I know I would sure rather be the patient than the spectator—you feel protected in a hospital bed—but when you're watching someone else in pain you feel like there is nothing you can do to help them.

Torey: One of my friends decided to have her hair cut for locks of love. It was a gesture she was making in my honor, and I went with her to the hairdresser's. My friend began crying because she couldn't bear the thought of cutting her hair. It was hard for me to understand how a completely healthy person whose hair would grow back could be so ridiculous. I told her: "I have to leave. Call me later when you can go through with this—I just cannot sympathize with you at all!" But then I also knew this woman who had breast cancer. She named her little dog Torey! She would talk to the dog and say, "If Torey can get through this, I can!" She thought I was an inspiration!

After you were diagnosed with cancer, what were the times when you felt the most "normal"?

Bethany: I always felt a lot more normal at night when everybody would come home from school and work. At that time of day everybody was flopped down on the couch unwinding, so I didn't feel like I was different from anybody else then.

Torey: I used to go to bed and try to tell myself this was all a big dream and that life would go back to normal when I woke up.

Aibjah: Usually between the hours of about 3:00 and 5:00 AM I would just lie in bed and bounce. I would come up with these outrageous ideas—sort of like dreaming while you are awake. I would design a building in my mind or make these massive, detailed plans to do something and talk to my dad about implementing them the next day. He would just look at me, shake his head, and ask me where I came up with this stuff!

Bethany: I dream a lot about running again—I was never really very athletic and I didn't run a lot before I got sick, but now that I need a total hip replacement it makes me sad to know I'll never be able to run again. It's something I really took for granted!

How has cancer affected your family relationships?

Torey: I have a brother who is eleven months older than I am. When I was first diagnosed my family was told that I wasn't going to make it, so my parents spent a lot of time with me in the hospital. My brother didn't come with them very much and he started getting into trouble.

Abijah: A lot of my parents' time and attention were directed toward me during my treatment, which was difficult for my sister. I've tried to make it up to her by forgoing plans of my own, like going to Camp Good Days and Special Times, so that I could go to her graduation and cheerleading meets.

Bethany: My sister and I are five years apart. When I was diagnosed she was only ten, so our relationship really changed a lot. When we had fights before I got sick she used to beat the crap out of me—but when I got cancer it was hands off! She couldn't understand why I couldn't do all the things I used to. I was admitted to the hospital several times because of complications, and my mom always stayed with me in the hospital, so that was hard on her too. There was definitely a lot of jealousy.

Kim: My sister [who was 16] would come to see me every day in the hospital when I was in for the first month of induction. She would lie on the bed and cry with me. She said she would shave her hair off too, but I told her she didn't have to. My mom would try to spend time with her when I passed out, but I think she was old enough to understand. I think I still probably expect a little too much of my parents' attention, even now!

As the young people talked, sometimes topics came up that even other cancer survivors are

What Is Induction?

The first phase of treatment for a patient with a blood cancer like leukemia is called **induction therapy**. It may include chemotherapy or radiation therapy, and it is designed to destroy a maximum number of blood cancer cells in order to eradicate any signs or effects of the disease (remission).

Coping with Bethany's cancer was often difficult for her sister Abby. At the time this picture was taken, Bethany was in the intensive care unit with blood clots in her heart. Their parents gave Abby the choice of going to a party with her friends after her elementary school graduation—or back to the hospital with them. As Abby struggled with her decision, she turned the camera on herself and snapped this picture. She so much wanted to be with her friends, but she was also terribly aware of her sister's situation. Ultimately, she decided to go back to the hospital.

reluctant to ask. Bethany, a little hesitantly, decided to ask Abijah and Torey a question that had been on her mind: "Do you ever feel like you have to stay with your partner or mate because they stood by you while you went through treatment?" Torey admits that she has wondered if her boyfriend found it difficult to think about breaking up with her while she was undergoing treatment for fear of what it would do to her. "Is it unfair to him, knowing that my cancer might come back? What if we choose to have children? What will it do to them? Should he find another girlfriend? I told him he didn't have to do this: 'I have to, but you don't. If you don't feel you can handle it, we should break up.' What if I hadn't gotten sick? Would our relationship have changed?" Abijah told his girlfriend the same thing: "'We can still be friends.' If I had not gotten cancer I might have lived on campus and maybe things would have changed." Things weren't different though, and situations have played out the way they have. Torey and Abijah are both emphatic in their feeling that things are as they should be, and that what they have shared and the bonds they have formed have created relationships of a strength and intimacy that might not exist otherwise.

From this topic the discussion easily transitioned to marriage, family, and children. Bethany received such intensive chemotherapy that many of her hormones have been suppressed. She has not had a period in three years. "I used to wonder if I really wanted kids. But when faced with the possibility that I might not be able to, I decided I really do want them." She is currently being seen by an adolescent gynecologist in hopes that medication may restart her cycle. Meanwhile, because Torey received total body radiation and she reached the allowable limit for her lifetime, she will not be able to have children of her own. While this saddens her, it has also helped her to formulate very strong ideas about what she hopes for in life. Many people suggest adoption as an alternative and Torey bristles a little at this. "If adoption is 'not that bad' why don't you adopt?" she replies. While adoption is a wonderful solution for many families, she becomes a little impatient with how easily people offer up the idea as a suitable replacement for having a family of her own. She understands that people are trying to make her feel better, but says that "people don't really realize the impact of being told you will never bear your own children." Other infertile couples have many options to pursue such as fertility treatments or invitro fertilization, but for Torey there are no options. Torey has trained to be a teacher, and Bethany wondered if being around kids will be hard for her, to which she replied, "I would like whomever I end up marrying to have the opportunity to have his own children. I would consider using a surrogate mother or adopting." Abijah will be able to have children, but if his cancer returned, it could go to his brain, spine, or testicles, in which case he says he would bank sperm before having any treatments that could cause him to be infertile.

What would you tell kids who do not have cancer?

Bethany: Don't be afraid of the illness. You can't catch it. We are still people just like you. We still have thoughts and feelings. We just happen to have an illness that could kill us!"

Torey: And the medicine that is trying to fix it is trying to kill us too!

Kim: I have a good friend who would come over to visit and talk about her day and never ask me about my cancer. It would have made me feel better if she had. You know—this is my life right now. Ask me some questions. There has to be something you don't know or understand.

Bethany: I wonder what I would have done if I hadn't been the one—if someone else had been diagnosed. I probably would have been afraid to ask too because I doesn't like to upset people. It's kind of hard to think about.

Abijah: Ask questions if you don't understand. We won't be offended. Don't make snap judgments about us. I would rather have somebody ask me if I was going to die than just look at me and walk away, or tell someone else that I was going to die.

What would you tell kids that were just diagnosed?

Bethany: I wouldn't feed them any bull. They need to be told straight up what's going on and warned that they are in for one big roller coaster ride. They should be on their guard. I would also say to parents that you know your kids better than anyone. If your kid thinks there is something wrong get it checked out. Doctors aren't perfect, and if they don't seem to be hearing what you're saying, be persistent and push the issue until you are satisfied.

Has cancer left behind any special gifts for you?

Bethany: At first I was pretty disappointed in my body because I felt like it had somehow let me down. During treatment, when I was so sick, I had this feeling of being trapped in my body when my mind and my spirit were trying so hard to live. Later, I realized that I had to appreciate my body and be grateful that it hung in there and got me through so much. My body is kind of a wreck now, and I have stretch marks all over my back, chest, arms, and legs from steroids, but I will never be ashamed of it again. I think coming to that realization has been a real gift.

Kim: I would say I definitely have more direction. I tend to get more involved now when I am passionate about something. I did a presentation about young adults and adolescents with cancer for a college course I was taking. I talked about how there were plenty of programs and services for kids and adults with cancer, but a real lack of things designed just for teens or young adults. After the presentation I got a call from Gary Mervis, the guy who started Camp Good Days and Special Times after his daughter Teddi, who had been diagnosed with cancer, passed away. He said, "We want to make a retreat just for you guys [young adults]. The sky is the limit. What do you want to do?" So now every year they offer Young Adult camp week. People our age are going through so much psychologically, sexually, and socially. To think about the future and try to prepare for things like college can be overwhelming. You can get lost without other people to go through it with.

Torey: One of the great gifts cancer has left me is my relationship with my mom.

Abijah: I've made huge connections with the people I've met along the way. Torey has become one of my best friends.

End of treatment for these kids brings its own challenges. Even though it is a time for celebration all around, it is also a very bittersweet moment as they realize that they will be seeing much less of the people who have provided so much support and encouragement, and in a very real sense, saved their lives. Nurses and doctors become part of an extended family, and for a while they fill the void left by the loss of other relationships when kids can no longer participate as actively in school or other activities. Leaving the secure environment of the hospital is a bit like learning to walk unaided as they begin the next chapter of their lives.

Abijah describes his last day of treatment as happy, but sad. The nurses cried and his doctor was emotional too. Bethany says, "When my treatment ended I wished that I could have a relationship outside of the hospital with my doctors and nurses; you know, that we could hang out together, go on picnics, stuff like that. It was sad for me when treatment stopped and I realized that was the basis of our relationship. I know they care about me, but when it's time to step out on your own, to a certain extent you leave those relationships behind. It's healthy and realistic, but sad. They will always be an important part of my life though.

For Torey, the feelings are even more intense. Her eleven-year journey battling cancer has made it very hard for her to think about leaving Strong Hospital where she has received her treatment. It is her safe place and her emotional attachment is very strong.

She says she will never say good-bye to these people and will always go there, no matter where she lives or what her insurance is, even if she has to pay out of pocket to go there.

Unfortunately, the end of treatment doesn't mean the end of cancer-related challenges these survivors must face. In addition to the psychological and emotional impact of ending treatment are health problems referred to as "late effects" that are associated with different therapies. These side effects can appear months or even years down the road. Addressing these potential problems has become even more of a concern as survival rates have increased by 45 percent over the last forty years. Radiation to the brain can affect learning, memory, and other cognitive function, especially in the very young whose brains are continuing to develop. Treatment for some cancers can make individuals vulnerable to the development of secondary cancers. Certain chemotherapies can damage the heart as well as other organs. For this reason, lifelong monitoring of patient health is necessary through visits to Long-Term Survivor Clinics. This kind of follow up is also helpful in conducting research aimed at minimizing late effects.

Over and above the immediate concerns of physical well-being are fears about job discrimination, difficulties obtaining health insurance, and other legal issues. Some employers believe cancer survivors may be less productive on the job or that they may have excessive absenteeism. Protection against this kind of discrimination is available under the Federal Rehabilitation Act of 1973, which states that federal employers or companies receiving federal funds cannot discriminate against handicapped workers, including cancer survivors, as well as under the Americans with Disabilities Act. Survivors can also learn about their rights from sources such as their local American Cancer Society and the National Coalition for Cancer Survivorship.

Chapter Eight
THE PEOPLE WHO HELP SURVIVORS SURVIVE

Who are the outside helpers who aid these young people as they wage their war on a silent, unseen enemy? They are many and varied, from family and friends to health care professionals, social workers, and child life specialists who work in hospitals. The bonds forged with a doctor, that one special nurse, or the clinic secretary who has become such a familiar, friendly face become very strong indeed.

DOCTORS WHO MAKE A DIFFERENCE

Bethany says of her primary oncologist: "I just love Dr. Korones! I have so much respect for

Bethany's oncologist, Dr. Korones.

him, not just because of the knowledge and power he has to make me well, but because he listens to me and makes me feel good about myself." Her mom makes the observation that "he seems to be very humbled by the position he is in. My impression is that he feels very privileged to be caring for these kids and that talking to them is one of the most rewarding parts of his job." Their perceptions are pretty much on the mark. An excerpt from an article written by Dr.

Korones called "Taking Time" published in the *Journal of Clinical Oncology* states:

> Just as we ferret out clues about their illnesses, we must cast the line far and deep into the stream to learn about our patients' lives and to find out what makes them tick. This is as important as filling in all the little boxes on the "history and physical" forms that federal law mandates. It gives us a fuller context, and helps us to more fully understand the impact of our interventions on our patients' lives. More important than that, it establishes a human connection, providing an acknowledgment from us that their lives have meaning. . . All we have to do is take the time to ask them what they are reading, what CD they are listening to, what they are doing this weekend, what television shows they are watching; to take the time to look at their vacation pictures and ask them where they are going next.
>
> We should share in our patients' triumphs. It does not have to be a graduation. Sometimes it's walking again. Sometimes it's finally getting back to school. Sometimes it's just living one more day. For each patient we care for, that triumph is a uniquely shaped and a specially wrapped gift. And even though we are all too busy, and we worry that it takes up too much of our time, part

of being a physician to our patients is to unwrap the gift before us and to savor its magical contents.

ORGANIZATIONS

Not only individuals offer their help to survivors; support is also available through local organizations such as the CURE Childhood Cancer Association, a nationally recognized organization started in Rochester, New York, in 1976. Begun by a group of parents who had lost children to cancer, it has become a model for childhood cancer groups across the nation. The acronym CURE stands for Counseling, Understanding, Resource, and Education, all needs that CURE has ably addressed. They have developed a *Parent Child Handbook* for newly diagnosed kids and their families that explains therapies, drugs, and side effects, and helps decode so much of the medical jargon that can seem so overwhelming. They also fund an educational liaison who visits schools to explain to students and teachers the special needs and limitations of a child undergoing treatment who may be returning to the classroom. The liaison ensures that every effort is made to procure any special accommodations available to the child as provided for under the law. The most noticeable support comes in the form of the ever-present parent advocate, Carol, herself a parent of a cancer survivor. She makes daily visits to the hospital, visiting both the inpatient floor and outpatient clinic to offer emotional support, acting as a critical go-between for parents and hospital staff, and sharing information about hospital procedures and community resources.

NURSES

If you visit the adolescent or pediatric floor of any hospital, it is quite likely your path will cross that of a nurse or another medical professional who won his or her own battle with cancer or some other serious disease, and later felt compelled to choose an occupation that would allow these individuals to "give back" a little of what they received. This is the case with Sonja, a nurse who was diagnosed with osteosarcoma as a child.

Now in her mid-forties, Sonja remembers her experience as vividly as though it were yesterday. It was Easter Sunday in the year 1973, and she was just eleven years old. When the family ran out of milk during dinner, Sonja volunteered to ride her bike to the local grocery store to get more. As she pedaled along, a pickup truck backed out of a driveway and struck her bike, knocking her to the ground. The vehicle had been concealed by another building that was situated closer to the road so Sonja was unable to see it until it was upon her. She recalls with amusement that the man driving the truck was actually the town drunk who never even noticed he had hit her. Sustaining no serious injuries beyond a bump or two, she hopped back on her bike and continued on to the grocery store. Possessing a flair for the dramatic, she made the most of the story upon returning home to the Easter celebration.

But the next day, Sonja's left femur was still a little painful so her mom took her to the doctor for an X-ray to rule out any broken bones. After reviewing the X-ray, the doctor called them back and asked them to come in for some additional X-rays; he had noticed a shadow at the very top of the film. Thinking the shadow was simply a cyst, he scheduled surgery for the day after Father's Day. However, a frozen section biopsy performed during the operation soon revealed it to be a rare subtype of osteosarcoma.

Why Is Your Blood Count Important When You're Being Treated for Cancer?

When your immune system is suppressed it means that your total white blood cell count is less than 1,000. This condition is known as neutropenia. The white blood cell count is made up of infection-fighting cells called polys and bands (young white blood cells). It is referred to as the absolute neutrophil count (ANC). These counts, along with hematocrit (volume of oxygen-carrying red blood cells) and platelet (clotting cells in the blood) counts are very important to monitor on a regular basis for kids undergoing the treatment for cancer, which unfortunately destroys healthy cells along with the abnormal cancerous ones.

Rather than undergoing limb-salvage surgery, the technique described in Brittany's case, Sonja's femur was carved down to the bone marrow in a crescent shape, and her leg placed in a splint that she wore until her return to school in the fall. In addition to surgery, Sonja took oral chemotherapy medication. Because her family could not afford this medication, her doctor generously purchased it himself from the nearby Roswell Cancer Institute and administered it to her in his own office.

She also received radiation to her leg (though this is now known to have no therapeutic value in treating osteosarcoma). Sonja remembers going for what she believed were routine X-rays (but were actually radiation treatments) to be sure her leg was healing properly, first every day for a week and gradually becoming less frequent until they ceased. "My mom definitely kept a lot of things secret from me" she says, "which was probably good for me at the time." She admits that this is in opposition to the philosophy held by most doctors today who believe they should be honest and upfront with kids: "You can lose their trust easily if they find out something they have been told isn't true or that you are keeping something from them. And if you hide something from them they will think the worst."

Confined to a wheelchair and later using crutches, Sonja remembers that the most disappointing thing for her was missing Field

What Is Biofeedback?

During biofeedback, instruments are used to measure a person's blood pressure, muscle tension, or heart rate. Information about these biological processes is "fed back" to the person in the form of a paper readout, lights, or beeps. The patient learns to use relaxation exercises to control the biological responses, such as imagining a peaceful place until his or her heart rate slows down. The techniques that are most effective at controlling the responses can be used even when the individual is no longer hooked up to the machine.

Days at the end of the school year and being unable to play outside all summer. "I didn't really understand how serious it was, and your priorities are definitely different as a kid."

Sonja attributes her early diagnosis and full recovery to divine intervention. "Just how it happened on Easter and the way it happened—If I hadn't been knocked off my bike it might not have been found until it was too late!" Because they lived in a small town, word eventually leaked out about the way her cancer was discovered. The man responsible for hitting Sonja came to the house to apologize, but her parents assured him no apology was needed; in fact, they felt they should be thanking him! If the accident had never happened, they might never have known until too late that Sonja had cancer.

Sonja knew soon after her recovery that she would be involved in medicine in some way. She smiles when she remembers that in her eleven-year-old mind she was convinced she would find the cure for cancer. "I just knew that it had to be something simple that everyone was overlooking!" She may not have found the cure for cancer, but she has certainly found her niche working with kids in pediatrics. "My favorite patients are the long-term patients like kids being treated for cancer or other chronic illnesses like cystic fibrosis. You get to know them and their families so well. It feels good to know you're doing something positive for them, and you get so much in return. I know they say you shouldn't get close to your patients, but you can't *not* get close to them."

HELPING THE WHOLE PERSON

Sonja's words echo the sentiments expressed by Dr. Korones in his article. The oncologist often visits the floor where Sonja works. "I can't tell you how many times I've walked into a patient's room and heard him talking with him or her," Sonja says, "and it has nothing to do with the kid's treatment or illness. He'll be asking them questions about what they would like to be when they get older, where they'd like to go to college. He helps them look into the future and believe that they *will have* a future." This kind of connection, she believes, is as important as any medicine, as is the very real power of positive thinking.

Sonja also believes educating kids about their illness is a wonderful tool that empowers them in battling their disease. Kids with cancer need to keep track of their blood counts and the terminology can sound pretty confusing. When she has the opportunity, Sonja likes to explain things in terms they can understand. For example, she likens segs and bands, which are adult white blood cells, to grownups who have a job, drive a car, and pay the bills. "Monocytes," she says, "are teenagers who can do a lot of those same things, but they don't have the money to do them. They can drive a car, but they don't have the money for gas—they have to get it from the adults. They will be adults real soon. Blasts (which are immature cells that multiply out of control in cancers like acute lymphoblastic leukemia) are like NICU (neonatal intensive care unit) babies. We don't want them out yet."

When kids are bothered by mouth sores or upset about the hair loss that accompanies chemotherapy, Sonja is quick to point out

Living—Really Living

It's been more than 5 years since my double-lung transplant and I have accomplished so much. . . . Sure, I've had some setbacks, including a couple of hospitalizations. But I apply the same attitude I always have: Think positive, do what's needed to get better, and move on.

that while these side effects may be trouble-some, they are only temporary, and in fact are indications their treatment is doing what it is supposed to do: destroy rapidly reproducing cells like cancer cells. Hair and skin cells reproduce quickly as well and therefore are vulnerable to chemotherapy, which makes the skin fragile, and body hair (including that on the scalp, leg, pubic area, eyebrows, and even eyelashes) fall out. Sonja believes this knowledge, coupled with the positive thinking she mentions and other mind-body therapies like counseling, biofeedback, **visualization**, and meditation can definitely play a role in the healing of patients with cancer.

SURVIVORS WHO CHANGE THE WORLD

There are many kinds of survivors in the world—but something many of them have in common is that they are people with trans-formed lives and views of the world. As they enter adulthood they frequently channel what they have learned into choosing occupations designed to help others engaged in the same struggle, either through professions in the medical field, or in jobs like social work, which includes child life specialists, and music and art therapists who offer kids important out-lets for expression as they navigate their jour-ney. Others volunteer their time and effort to organizations that reach out to families with emotional support, or sometimes in more

visualization: *is a way of using your imagination to create mental images that help you to achieve a state of relaxation or well-being.*

tangible ways by volunteering at facilities like the Ronald McDonald House.

Nearly all of the teens interviewed in this book live in the area surrounding Rochester, New York, and have been campers at Camp Good Days and Special Times, a camp for kids diagnosed with cancer and other life-threatening illnesses. It was founded in 1979 by Gary Mervis when his own daughter Teddi was diagnosed with a malignant brain tumor, Located on Keuka Lake in New York State, it gives kids "the opportunity to regain some of their lost childhood." Drawing upon their own experiences, kids like Torey, Brittany, Kim, Mike, and Abijah have volunteered as counselors and find themselves uniquely able to serve as strong and sympathetic sounding boards; after all, they've "been there." The camp's fun activities can be geared to a child's specific needs and abilities and present welcome distractions from the realities of dressing changes, catheters, ports, and IV bags.

Several of the teens whose stories are included in this book have agreed to sit on

Ronald McDonald House

A readily recognized household name, the Ronald McDonald House has locations throughout the nation and in fifty-one countries that provide families a "home away from home" allowing them to be close to their children while they receive medical treatment. Volunteers spend time with family members, prepare meals, take children on outings, and help with fundraising.

panels at conferences and symposiums that address doctors, nurses, social workers, and other health care professionals in an effort to help them improve treatments and better understand, serve, and relate to the needs of kids stricken with cancer. By telling their stories, they help other kids who face the same challenges.

Survivors know that life is precious. Maybe that's why so many of them work so hard to make life better for us all.

People taking part in a cancer walk demonstrate their support for cancer research. Many of the walkers are also cancer survivors.

Living with Cystic Fibrosis

Grant's Story, from the Nemour Foundation's TeensHealth Web site, kidshealth.org

I was diagnosed with cystic fibrosis (CF) when I was 7 months old. I am now 23. People with CF produce an abnormally thick mucus that clogs the respiratory and digestive systems. This congestion can lead to serious and frequent lung infections. Also, the body doesn't produce the natural enzymes needed for digestion of food and absorption of nutrients.

All these things can cause CF to take quite a toll on a person's energy level. Luckily, I take enzymes by mouth so I can digest everything I eat. But I still had a very poor appetite as a kid and teen. I liked to eat; I just didn't eat much. So to get the right amount of calories per day, I had a feeding tube placed on top of my skin and attached to my stomach. Through this tube, I received a high-calorie, nutritional liquid during the night while I slept.

By the time I was 13, my cystic fibrosis was getting progressively worse. I got more and more lung infections and was in the hospital more often. I always fought back, recovered, and got back to my "normal" life. But eventually, the constant setbacks took their toll. My hospitalizations became more frequent, and I missed more days of school.

NOT YOUR NORMAL HIGH-SCHOOL UPS AND DOWNS

Quite frankly, I was nervous about going into high school. Not only was I entering a new school and

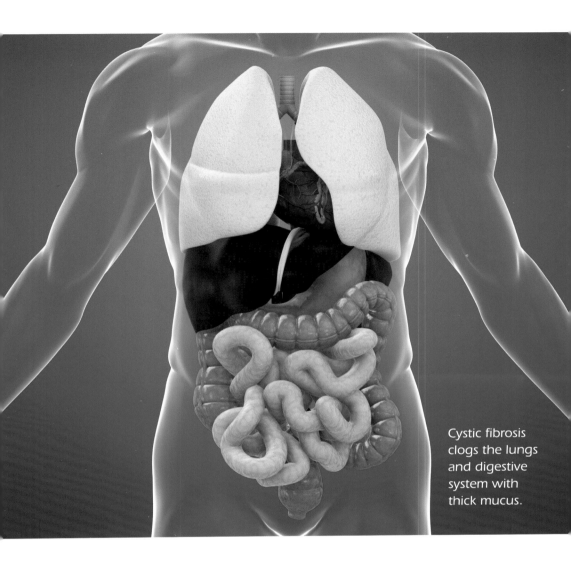

Cystic fibrosis clogs the lungs and digestive system with thick mucus.

environment, I also knew my health was slowly getting worse. It was hard for me to do simple things, even carry books and walk to class. . . .

One of the best things to do for CF is to get active. Physical activities such as basketball, tennis, or running get the lungs working hard and can help clear extra mucus. Unfortunately, one of the last things I felt like doing in high school was running or playing a sport. Now that I exercise more and feel the benefits, I wish I had pushed myself to exercise more. It probably would have helped.

In the 9th grade I walked by the yearbook staffroom every day. They always looked like they were having fun. So in 10th grade, I applied to be on the staff and was accepted. It turned out to be the best thing for me during high school.

Everybody was so cool and had a great attitude toward my CF (mostly because I did, too). When I was having a "bad" day, they understood and gave me assistance if I needed it. The yearbook staff was my support group and just knowing they had my back helped me get through a lot of tough times.

It's wonderful to have friends around when you're feeling sick or even a little scared. I made incredible friends in school, often through getting involved in clubs, and I still keep in touch with many of them today. A few of them even told me they learned a lot from me about being positive and strong. . . .

By my junior year, my CF was getting pretty bad and my stamina was even worse. My doctors recommended that I only stay at school for half a day and do my other subjects through home schooling. I was pretty psyched to get to leave school early every day, but found I missed out on a lot. It gave me more time to rest, eat, and do all of my CF treatments. But I missed my time with my friends. . . .

When I was 16, I was told that I would need a double-lung transplant if I wanted to survive. It would be a huge operation. But I knew that I wanted it because I wasn't done living. I had more to do and this was going to give me the power to do it. After my surgery, I came back home . . . able to walk, without oxygen or assistance, in my high school graduation.

I still have cystic fibrosis, but now it's only in my digestive system. The transplant gave me lungs that do not have CF and never will. After the lung transplant, I was able to take long, deep breaths and had tons more energy and stamina. My appetite went from hardly eating to eating everything. My body needed more fuel now that it was running on all cylinders! My feeding tube was removed about a year after my transplant. I was really glad about that!

Chapter Nine

WHAT DOES IT MEAN TO BE A SURVIVOR?

Not all stories have happy endings. Not every young person who fights a serious disease wins his or her battle. Those who are left behind have their own stories to tell.

As anyone who has ever had a loved one stricken with cancer will tell you, when that individual is diagnosed with cancer the whole family has cancer. The disease has far-reaching implications for all those who are close to that person. In addition to the very real, gut-wrenching fear that descends upon them are the effects on siblings who may be unintentionally and unavoidably sidelined. When someone loses his battle with cancer, loved ones and family members are in a very real sense the ones who have survived the incredible ordeal of the disease.

LAUREN'S STORY

This is the case with Lauren Spiker, the mother of Melissa, who was diagnosed at the age of seventeen with a rare malignancy of the bone marrow called Myelodysplastic Syndrome. Melissa was a young woman of exceptional intelligence, talent, and a passion for living that remained undiminished throughout her difficult treatment. Twice she was declared to be in remission, and twice she relapsed. In spite of aggressive chemotherapy, total body radiation with a bone marrow transplant, and brain seizures that resulted in partial paralysis and loss of speech, Melissa never gave up her dream of attending the University of Pennsylvania to pursue a nursing degree. Unable to travel far from home, she took classes locally at the University of Rochester, where she earned a perfect 4.0 in spite of weakness and difficulty with neurological function.

As her condition seemed to improve, she made plans to finally attend the University of Pennsylvania in January of 2000. After another bone marrow biopsy revealed that she had once again relapsed, Melissa bravely continued with her plan, telling her parents, "If I don't go now, I never will." In spite of daily blood transfusions and frequent trips to the emergency room, Melissa carried on with her studies, participating in daily student life, as well as undergoing experimental treatments in a last effort to bring her disease under control. While at UPenn she touched many lives, earning the admiration and respect of those around her.

A final biopsy however, showed that the treatment had not been successful. Melissa decided to stop all treatment and return home to savor every last moment of her remaining time with family and friends, but not before being awarded an honorary Bachelor of Science in Nursing in a rare tribute from the university. Afterward, in her honor, the University established the Melissa Sengbusch Inspiration Scholarship, for which Melissa proudly established the eligibility criteria.

Upon her return home Melissa took a glorious vacation with her family to the Grand Canyon, rode a hot air balloon over the Arizona desert, planted an herb garden, crocheted an afghan, and took a pottery class at the local art gallery, all while writing profound poetry and prose in her journal. She said good-bye to her friends and family. She made plans for her death and burial, donating her body for medical study. Before she died, she asked a promise of her mother. "If you have learned anything from me through all of this, do something with it to make a difference—to make things better."

Lauren promised—and she has kept her word. In the years since her daughter's death, she has established Melissa's Living Legacy Foundation, which sponsors the comprehensive Web site she created called Teens Living with Cancer. This site gives teens diagnosed

Teens Living With Cancer

All Lauren's efforts focus on several needs confronting teens living with cancer. She has identified these on the Teens Living with Cancer Web site:

- physical changes and/or disfigurement when appearance is a paramount concern
- loss of peer group and acceptance when inclusion is a primary need
- reproductive challenges and sexual dilemmas at a time of emerging sexuality
- unsolicited dependence at a time of newfound independence
- loss of control when new boundaries are just being tested

Melissa's Living Legacy Foundation is dedicated to bridging this gap in service.

with cancer, as well as their families, an opportunity to interact with one another in the form of discussion boards and also offers a valuable medical resource for friends, family, and health care professionals. She also developed an interactive CD-ROM called Cancer 101—Straight Talk from Teens that provides tips about dealing with cancer.

The Teens Living with Cancer Web site receives thousands of hits each day, and Cancer 101 has been distributed in countries all over the world. Each year, Lauren hosts an elegant dinner followed by a silent auction featuring items donated by local individuals and corporations who support her cause. She is always joined in this effort by a group of devoted teens who participate in some way in the program of the evening, which focuses attention on the goals of Teens Living with Cancer. In addition, each year an individual is selected and presented with the Melissa's Living Legacy "Make a Difference" Award. Honoring the memory of her daughter has made all the difference for thousands of teens and given Lauren a true sense of purpose and fulfillment.

FACING DEATH

As this book was being written, the young people who have shared their stories here were called upon to face the unthinkable: losing a member of their own group after his relapse. As brave, determined, and full of hope as they all are, and as familiar as they are with grief, their friend's relapse has left them angry, struggling with denial, and filled with terror for their friend and themselves. They were especially shaken since, for them, their friend had always been a symbol of hope and a source of encouragement after beating back his disease during an earlier relapse. He was filled with a joy for living, and possessed a terrific sense of humor and a spark that always ignited the rest of the group.

The kids met recently to comfort one another and decide how best to offer comfort and support to their friend. The room was silent as they struggled with their emotions and tears began to flow. Drawing upon her own experience, Lauren Spiker, Melissa's mom and the founder of Teens Living with Cancer, put into words what everyone else felt but didn't know how to say: "I think the best way we can honor our friend is to let him know that his life meant something, that he was here for a purpose, which he served very well, that we love him, and we'll never forget him!" A decision was made to record a video with greetings and messages from everyone. Another suggestion was made to fill an empty bottle with handwritten notes tied to a slender ribbon that could be pulled out one at a time and read. The young man courageously and generously agreed to be videotaped as he lived out his last days, as a gesture of love to those he leaves behind and to educate the rest of us about the horrors of a disease like cancer—but also to celebrate the resilience of the human spirit.

ALL OF US ARE SURVIVORS

The kids who told their stories for this book have faced cancer. Other people deal with other diseases, and still others face the effects of catastrophic accidents that have damaged their bodies. We can't really compare these events; we can't say one is worse than the

other, for in the end, each person must bear his or her pain. Whether we are speaking of a mother in Africa who has survived war, famine, and AIDS . . . a child in Iraq whose family was killed in the war . . . an elderly man in New York City whose daughter was killed

Melissa Spiker told her mother, "If you have learned anything from me through all of this, do something with it to make a difference—to make things better."

in the 9/11 terrorist attack . . . or a teenager who struggles to cope with the challenges of daily life, we are all called upon to face the circumstances of our lives and deal with them creatively in some way.

This means that whatever we face, we refuse to let events limit who we are on the inside or what we have to offer the world. We take even the worst pain and use it creatively, to reach out to others; to inspire music, paintings, poetry, and stories; to challenge ourselves to play sports, make gardens, invent new things, research new scientific discoveries; to make ourselves stronger. We live with hope and courage, taking pleasure in life's many joys, no matter how much hurt we are asked to endure.

In the end, none of us gets to choose how and when we will die. But we are all survivors until we reach that moment when we draw our last breath. Maybe it is when we contemplate how we may die that we learn best how we should live.

Surviving Asthma

Samantha's Story, from the
Nemour Foundation's
TeensHealth Web site,
kidshealth.org

I remember my very first asthma attack, only I had no idea what was going on at the time. As a little kid you are always trying to keep up with everyone around you, so it's fairly common to be out of breath. For this reason, I never really recognized my asthma until I started taking swimming lessons twice a week. I complained to my instructor that the water was pushing on my chest or that my bathing suit was too tight. My complaints were dismissed; people just thought I was whining. What everyone failed to realize was that I was suffering from symptoms of asthma.

SCORING A DIAGNOSIS

I was eventually diagnosed with allergies and was treated weekly with allergy shots. Around this time, I started to play competitive soccer and my breathing problems resurfaced. But this time they were much more intense. On any sports team, every individual is expected to play his or her hardest. Every time I stepped onto the playing field, I was there to do my best. It didn't matter if I was the best player or the very worst; I just wanted to play the game. I started to suffer from breathing problems again, and to be honest, they gave me a feeling of inferiority, of weakness, so I tried to play through them.

Unfortunately, this led to several attacks that were a bit more severe than the ones I endured in swimming. Obviously, something was wrong. I was fit and relatively athletic, but still having difficulty breathing.

From this point on, my occasional asthma attacks at soccer grew much more frequent and severe. Instead of just losing my breath or experiencing mild wheezing, I had a loud, choking-like wheeze. I was on the border of passing out many times. Still, I didn't want to be weak. I wanted to show I could endure anything. So I insisted that everything was OK, that I didn't need to see a doctor, that it was just a little cold, anything I could think of.

I started to suffer from a chronic cough, a wheezy, dry cough that just wouldn't go away. Finally, my parents insisted I see a doctor. This time my physician gave me a daily pill I would take to help prevent my asthma symptoms. In addition to that, I would take my fast-acting inhaler every 4 to 6 hours until the cough subsided. This seemed to work OK until a month later. I had a reaction to someone's perfume in French class. Coming into contact with things like strong perfume, the dander on pets, or pollen in the air can trigger a reaction in some people with asthma. Cigarette smoke is especially terrible for me—one whiff and I start coughing up a storm.

In this case, the perfume triggered my asthma and I started coughing and wheezing uncontrollably. My French teacher was trying to explain the imperfect tense of verbs as my vision blurred and the room started to spin. Next thing I knew, I was being hauled out on a stretcher and into an ambulance.

I have never been so frightened in my life. I don't even remember a lot of what happened because I kept coming in and out of consciousness. I remember lying on the floor, I remember someone asking me where my inhaler was, and I remember a teacher telling me, "It's all going to be all right, it's going to be just fine, just breathe." It wasn't until I was in the ambulance that I really came out of my baffled state and my breathing stabilized.

Once I got to the hospital I was put on a nebulizer, which is a device used to change liquid medication into something a person can breathe. It consists of a mouthpiece, tubing, and the compressor (which changes the state of the medication from liquid to vapor). After being released with a referral to see my usual physician, I made my way home. . . .

TAKING CONTROL

Now, in addition to the fast-acting inhaler I've always used, I take another inhaler every day as a preventive medication, along with my daily pill. Before I play sports, during an attack, or if I have a wheezing cough, I take the fast-acting inhaler. To be honest I am not too fond of that fast-acting inhaler—it makes me jittery and shaky and hyper. But I do what I need to do in order to stay as healthy as I can. . . .

I think that playing sports has really helped me with my asthma. Playing a sport increases your lung capacity, and physical fitness is incredibly important to a person with asthma. . . . Within the last year I started running track as an in-between sport for soccer to keep in shape and get some good exercise. I never would have guessed that I would fall in love with the sport so quickly. This past fall I switched from soccer to cross-country for the first time, where I found it was much easier to control my asthma. . . .

As much as I love running, it gets frustrating sometimes. Days when I want to run more, I want to run faster, but I just can't breathe are the worst. But I work through them to the best of my ability. Sometimes it feels like every time I run it's a struggle between me and my breath. That last stretch is always the most grueling part of the race and the hardest test of my asthma. I just focus on that finish line and sprint with every fiber of my being, knowing that the end is just a few more strides away.

The burst of exhilaration and pride that fills me when I cross that line is almost indescribable. It surpasses anything I have ever experienced in soccer; I guess it must be what some call a "runner's high." This experience, asthma, running, everything, has taught me what it means to want something and to work for it, using every possible resource to get to where I need to be. I know now that what I once thought was a weakness has made me stronger, and knowing this has made all of the trials and tests worth it.

Further Reading

Dodd, Mike. *Oliver's Story: A book for Sibs of Kids with Cancer*. Kensington MD: Candle-lighters Childhood Cancer Foundation, 2004.

Gootman, Marilyn E., author. Pamela Espe-land, ed. *When a Friend Dies: A Book for Teens About Grieving & Healing*. Free Spirit Publishing, 1994.

Keene, Nancy, Wendy Hobbie and Kathy Ruccione. *Childhood Cancer Survivors: A Practical Guide to Your Future* (Patient Centered Guides). O'Reilly, 2006.

Mareck, Amy M. *Fighting For My Life: Growing up with Cancer*. Fairview Press, 2007.

National Research Council, author. Maria Hewitt, Susan L. Weiner and Joseph V. Simone, eds. *Childhood Cancer Survivorship: Improving Care and Quality of Life*. The National Academies Press, 2003.

Steen, R. Granta and Joseph Mirro, authors, eds. *Childhood Cancer: A Handbook from St. Jude Children's Research Hospital*. Da Capo Press, 2000.

White, P. Gill, PhD. *Sibling Grief: Healing After the Death of a Sister or Brother*. iUniverse, Inc., 2006.

Woznick, Leigh A. and Carol D. *Goodheart Living With Childhood Cancer: A Practical Guide to Help Families Cope*. American Psychological Association (APA), 2001.

For More Information

Abramson Cancer Center of the University of Pennsylvania
http://www.oncolink.upenn.edu/index.cfm
Using this cancer resource, one can gather information pertaining to cancer types, treatment, or how to cope if you or a loved one has cancer. Also provides many alternate resources to research the disease.

American Cancer Society
www.cancer.org

A nationwide health organization centered on the fight against cancer. Along with cancer advocacy and information, this website includes numerous message boards where anyone is free to discuss their questions, concerns, or experiences dealing with cancer.

Association of Cancer Online Resources
www.acor.org
This is a free online resource for everyone affected by cancer. Provides information on treatment options and types of cancer, along with 159 mailing lists that offer help and support to those in need.

Cure Childhood Cancer Association
www.curekidscancer.com
Provides peer support for families with children who have either cancer or a blood disorder. Helps children and their families deal with the both the immediate effects of cancer, and their continuing lives after cancer.

For More Information

Locks of Love
www.locksoflove.org
A non-profit organization that takes donated hair and uses it to create hairpieces. These are then provided to financially disadvantaged children who are afflicted by long-term hair loss as a result of any medical diagnosis.

National Cancer Institute
www.cancer.gov
Government run site that deals with cancer research, funding, statistics, and other useful information.

National Childhood Cancer Foundation
www.nccf.org
Childhood cancer research organization who's goal is to cure and prevent childhood cancer through research.

National Coalition for Cancer Survivorship
www.canceradvocacy.org
Site for the oldest cancer advocacy organization, in the United States, that is led by survivors. Along with educating patients, the NCCS works towards causing changes to take place in the federal level to improve how we research, finance, and provide cancer care.

For More Information

Teens Living with Cancer (TLC)
www.teenslivingwithcancer.org
Inspired Melissa Marie Sengbusch, a nineteen year old who died of cancer, this is a resource and guide for kids and teens who are living with cancer. Includes tips on staying healthy, true life stories, and facts about cancer.

Publisher's note:
The Web sites listed on these pages were active at the time of publication. The publisher is not responsible for Web sites that have changed their addresses or discontinued operation since the date of publication. The publisher will review and update the Web-site list upon each reprint.

Bibliography

American Cancer Society. http://www.cancer.org/docroot/home/index.asp.

Brown, Pamela N. *Facing Cancer Together.* Minneapolis, Minn.: Augsburg Fortress, 2000.

DeVita, Vincent T., Theodore S. Lawrence, and Steven A. Rosenberg. *Cancer: Principles & Practice of Oncology.* Philadelphia, Penn.: Lippincott Williams & Wilkins, 2008.

Givler, Amy. *Hope in the Face of Cancer.* Eugene, Ore.: Harvest House, 2003.

The Lung Association. "Faces of Asthma." http://www.lung.ca/diseases-maladies/asthma-asthme/faces-visages/katie_e.php/.

National Cancer Institute. http://www.cancer.gov/.

Nemours Foundation. Kids' Health. http://kidshealth.org/teen/diseases_conditions/. Weinberg, Robert A. *The Biology of Cancer.* London: Garland Science, 2006.

Index

Dreamstime
  Anette Romanenko: p. 15
  Duplass, Jamie: p. 8
  Eraxion: p. 10, 45, 65, 100
  Jblko: p. 31
  Jcka: p. 49
  Li, Wa: p. 23
  Photawa: p. 107
  Ron Chapple Studios: p. 91

Jupiter Images: p. 108

Spiker, Lauren: p. 115

Therrien, Patricia: p. 18, 27, 28, 32, 35, 39, 41, 52, 56, 58, 61, 66, 73, 81, 92

Vet Cancer Care: p. 63

About the Author and the Consultant

Author

Patricia Therrien lives in upstate New York with her husband, three children, four cats, two dogs, and three horses. Her teenaged daughter was diagnosed with cancer in January of 2005 and is currently in remission.

Patricia would like to extend special thanks to the doctors, nurses, and staff at Golisano Children's Hospital at Strong whose dedicated service and unfailing compassion have made these survivor stories possible, and to Lauren Spiker, founder of *Teens Living with Cancer*, for helping kids with cancer find their voice.

Consultant

Andrew M. Kleiman, M.D. is a Clinical Instructor in Psychiatry at New York University School of Medicine. He received a BA in philosophy from the University of Michigan, and graduated from Tulane University School of Medicine. Dr. Kleiman completed his internship, residency, and fellowship in psychiatry at New York University and Bellevue Hospital. He is currently in private practice in Manhattan and teaches at New York University School of Medicine.